IN THE FULLNESS OF TIME

From an unsettled Poland in the 1920s, immigrants come to America, strangers in their origins, but compatriots in their country of choice.

Their descendants find themselves fighting for Hürtgen Forest, inside Nazi Germany. In December 1944, a strange truce brings medics from both sides together in harmony to save lives, during one of the most brutal battles of the war.

An impetuous gift is made, from one side to the other, that eventually is willed to a professor. He thinks little of it, until he stumbles upon a painting that prompts a journey of discovery, of an intertwining of lives, across generations, oceans, and wars.

JACK A. JARMON has taught international and global relations at the University of Pennsylvania and Rutgers University. In the mid 1990s he worked for the United States Agency for International Development as a technical advisor to the Russian government.

He has authored and co-authored five books, which are currently core texts for international and security studies programs in the US and abroad. "In the Fullness of Time" is his first novel.

Jack and his wife Barbara live with two Australian Shepherds. They (not the dogs) met in the 9th grade and started dating at the urging of their parents. Eventually, they married thirty-six years later.

In the Fullness of Time

Jack A. Jarmon

PERSEUBLISHING

PERSEUBLISHING

In the Fullness of Time

by Jack A. Jarmon, Ph.D.

Published by: Perseublishing, PO Box 181802, Coronado, California 92178, United States of America

FIC014050   FICTION / Historical / World War II
FIC019000   FICTION / Literary
FIC031050   FICTION / Thrillers / Military
FIC032000   FICTION / War & Military

1st paperback edition

ISBN: 9781951171179

Cover design by Bruce Oliver Newsome

Cover image is an excerpt from "A Time for Healing" (1996), watercolor/acrylic, painted by Robert Nisley (1919-2008), commissioned by the Pennsylvania Governor's Committee for World War II Commemoration, used with the permission of the Nisley family.

Chapters

Prologue: What is this Place?

Fifty miles south of Hamburg, a British officer and his aide reach their objective – a prison camp. Their exhaustion from days of battle and skirmishes still fresh, the two are about to confront a horror that would haunt them the rest of their lives. They are part of a relief force, and have driven through enemy territory and enemy fire to complete their mission. The operation is the result of an odd truce.

"What's that smell?"

"It smells like a monkey house, Sir. It's been getting stronger for the last 40 minutes."

The two men cannot ignore a sense of foreboding. As they move closer to their objective, a dread grotesqueness hangs in the air. After a quarter of an hour, their Tilly rolls to a halt a few yards from the perimeter. They reach the outer fence and dismount the car. As they move forward, the men are flushed with shock. They stagger.

"My God! What is this place!" breathes the sergeant.

Several days earlier, a Mercedes staff car with a white flag over its hood appeared on the horizon. Its occupants, two *Wehrmacht* colonels. Their destination, the British 159th Infantry Battalion's forward headquarters. They are suavely dressed with peaked caps and polished leather boots. They had come with a strange offer.

After being blindfolded, the men are taken back to the VIII Corps Headquarters for further interrogation. There, they make their proposal formal. A facility, across the British 11th Armoured Division's line of advance, is filled with detainees. They are sick with typhus. In order to prevent the disease from spreading, the Germans suggest a local truce to allow the British to take the camp. The *Wehrmacht* officers guarantee that until Allied troops arrive, the German and Hungarian guard units will remain in place. This is to stop any breakouts, which could result in an epidemic.

The British agree, but these colonels are acting autonomously and the area is still in German hands. To get there, they must fight their way through stubborn enemy resistance. The commanders muster troops for the assault force, while medical teams hastily organize. It takes over two days for the armored units to reach the outside wire.

After intense combat, the advance units finally arrive at the barriers to the enclosure. The two intelligence officers are among the first. From the outer perimeter of the camp, these men have no idea that what lies before them is a nightmare as inexpressible as it is incomprehensible.

Inside the camp are men, women, and children who have been starved and worked to death. Denied food and water for four days, a monstrous human swarm feeds off the internal organs of the dead who cover the ground like a carpet. Excrement, corpses, and rags stretch across the landscape. In the middle of this satanic phantasm, people gnaw on human limbs. Tens of thousands of former beings lie in grotesque shapes, several bodies deep. The expressions on their faces are as contorted as their limbs.

A Jewish chaplain would later try to comfort several young girls from Poland and Lithuania by leading them in song. But by the middle verses, he found himself weeping with his head on the table until the girls were able to reassure him.

Leslie Hardman, a Royal Army chaplain from Glynneath, Wales wrote:

> …almost as they emerged from the ground itself…a number of wraith-like creatures came tottering towards us. Their bodies from their heads to their feet looked like matchsticks. Two Tommies, entering the camp for the first time must have thought they had walked into a supernatural world. …They dropped their heavy sacks and fled.

"Sir, what is this place?" the sergeant asks his lieutenant.

"God only knows, Evans. All I can tell you is the nearest town is called Belsen."

1. The Old Barracks

The U.S. Army War College at Carlisle, Pennsylvania, is a complex of elderly stone barracks, snug apartments, and humble but well-kept administrative offices. It is part-Army base, part-college campus. Intimately nested in the rolling Cumberland Valley, the Barracks has stood since 1757, during the French and Indian War. Generations of American volunteers, farmers, immigrants, college boys, descendants of slaves, and professional soldiers have come here to learn how to wage war. They went to battlefields from North America to Europe, Asia, Africa, and the Mideast. Standing on this ground, you can sense their ghosts.

In one of the guest apartments, David Jergen is staring in the mirror a few feet away. The sight is saddening. Opposite is a man looking much older than his years. The sagging face reveals an exhaustion with life. Not long ago, it seemed, the jaw was square and the eyes wide with curiosity. But the onslaught of time left behind a sunken terrain. The aging professor places his hand on the wall for support while he rubs his stiffening neck muscles. After a few moments, he firms up his back. He takes from his pocket a rosary and places the tangled chain on the desk next to his computer. After a brief vacant stare, he makes his way toward the adjacent room.

Since arrival, Jergen has been pacing fitfully. The notes for his lecture remain unfinished on the desk as a picture in an adjoining room consumes him. It is a scene of American and German medical teams. Amid the combat, they share a desperate effort to save lives. While staring at the strokes, patterns, and dashes, he cannot resist searching for something he believes is hidden – a message. Could it be a warning, a presaging, or maybe a sign of hope? A curious mixture of exasperation and sorrow is overtaking him. Emotionally, he feels trapped.

Above an overworked leather couch, the brass plaque on the picture frame reads "A Time for Healing." Dying and suffering men from both sides swirl in its center. Medics and surgeons frantically try to save their comrades. The colors in the picture, like the groans of the wounded, are intense but muted. You feel the agony and torment, and for a moment it chills your heart.

On the table beside the couch Jergen notices a frail bound memoir by an Army medic. The title is: *My Valley of the Shadow.* He opens to a random page:

> A few days ago, several men were rotated back to the battalion aid station for psychiatric observation and treatment. Among them were two assigned to collect wounded GIs from the front. One carried a bag of souvenir teeth, the other had a supply of sliced ears of German dead. Through this endless winter, the forest has been alive with feral dogs who feed on corpses seared and blistered by white phosphorous. The days are so terrible, I pray for darkness. The nights are so bad, I pray for daylight.

Jergen takes a deep breath. Gently, he closes the soldier's testament and places it back on the table. He looks back up at the image. In the background is a figure to which his eyes return. It's a GI lieutenant with a clipboard. In the grip of crisis, the artist captures the central essence of an American triage officer. It is a portrait of stoicism and stability. But David also senses an eerie shutter of familiarity. The academic can't help thinking that any moment, despite the whirl of chaos and agony, the man will suddenly turn his head and speak directly to him.

David's captivation is broken by a knock at the door.

"Professor Jergen? It's Carl Washburn."

An Army captain in his late twenties steps inside. His eyes are steady. Squared away is his gouge line and the battle ribbons on his blazer.

"How are you doing? I hope the room is up to standards. It's a different ambiance than what you probably are used to back at University of Pennsylvania."

"Different, but in a good way."

"There's a lot of interest in your lecture today, Dr. Jergen. I'll make the dinner plans for tonight. And I noticed your brother will be joining us."

David nods.

"I saw on his official invitation, he is Dr. Jergen, also?"

"Yes, a medical doctor, or what my father used to call 'a Dr. doctor'," says the PhD.

"And you're simply 'doctor'?"

The professor smiles and shrugs. "By the way, there's an interesting piece of art in the next room. I was wondering if you could tell me anything about it?"

They walk together into the anteroom and stand in front of the print. "I know that picture. It's a picture of the Kall River truce at Hürtgen Forest." Carl stops to recall what he remembers from his readings. "Hürtgen was one of the bloodiest battles of the war. A German general even said it was worse than anything he had seen at the eastern front. It was the longest battle on German soil, I believe," mutters Washburn.

"The killing was endless." He goes on. "Some US units suffered 100 percent casualties. There were divisions that had casualty rates of 150 percent among the officers. Neither side would give an inch. The lull was an odd occurrence. During the First World War, there were plenty of truces arranged to allow medical teams to tend to their wounded. I understand the ceasefires in World War II were rare. Most were unofficial. I even read that at the Kall, Americans and Germans were treating each other's men. You couldn't tell the uniforms apart anyway. They were covered with mud and blood. All that mattered was whether their hearts were beating."

"A rare outbreak …of humanity."

"Then, they went back to slaughtering one another."

As they discuss the picture, Washburn has on his mind another conversation. He remembers talking to a member of his squad who was getting treated for PTSD. Over a cup of coffee in an old battered diner, a few blocks from a VA hospital, his buddy said: "The problem is Carl, when you're over there…all you can think about is home. And when you are home, all you can think about is being over there… I just want a safe place to take my head."

After three tours in Iraq, Washburn often asks himself, "Is it the same? Does it matter which war or what era? Are there any 'safe places for your head' once you've been over there?"

Jergen restarts the conversation. "My father was in the Ardennes with the 78th Infantry Division. I only know that because of the regimental journal he kept in the library. He was a combat medic. That's why the print caught my interest. He never talked much about his combat experience. I guess they never do. My brother heard half the stories and I heard the other half. We did know he was MIA for a while. His Jeep and driver ran over a land mine when they were looking for wounded. A driver may have been killed, but my father was found by a British patrol and brought back to a field hospital."

"That's all you know about your father's war experience?"

"Most of his 'war stories' had more to do with Basic Training and Officer Candidate School."

Carl laughs.

"The one souvenir we have is a German medical field kit. I don't know the complete story behind it, but my brother does, I think. I can't remember ever seeing it, actually."

"Well this was the home of the Medical Corps School during World War II. Maybe your father passed through. We have a library and archives here, in addition to the museum. If you need any help we would be happy to set you up."

"Great. We will probably take you up on that".

"Well, I best be going and let you get settled in."

David escorts the captain to the door to show him out.

Alone, again, Dave Jergen stands at the window at his work desk. He tries to concentrate on his lecture. But the thought of the print lingers.

The rain from the previous day has passed on. He looks out at a vast country and marvels at the changing verdure. Yet, he cannot ignore the odd dissonance stirring within. Since he entered the old fort, some unexplained presence and an ineffable feeling of survivor guilt has loomed over him. But unlike the knowing silence of the soldier at the Kall River, Jergen's quiescence weighs him down.

Before resuming his work at the computer screen, the professor goes back to the anteroom to take one last glance at the print – looking for something he knows is there but cannot see.

2. Warsaw, 1921

In the hollow of Warsaw's Gdansk Train Station, eddies of litter whirl between waiting passengers. Travelers speak in restless tones. The low din of their voices echoes off the bare walls. It's March, and despite a cold steady breeze, a sense of composure bordering on contentment settles over the scattered crowd.

Eager ticket-holders sit on wooden benches, beside dozing station employees, as an atmosphere of calm hovers over small gatherings. Jews and gentiles mingle, hardly taking notice of one another. From their indifference, it would seem neither group is aware the other exists.

Suddenly, with the abruptness of a lightning bolt, the stillness is broken by hellish screams. Pleas for help and mercy thunder throughout the cavernous train station. In a once soundless corner on the platform, thugs are using sheep-sheers to cut the beard from an old Hassidic Jew. They take slabs off his face and laugh like fiends.

By the time onlookers comprehend the horror, the goons scramble down the stairs and into the maze of tangled streets. Behind, they leave their victim in a pool of his blood and groaning in agony. The customarily tranquil station squirms with revulsion.

Some bystanders run to the Hassidim's aid. Several try to staunch the bleeding. The majority are sickened and repulsed, while only a few react with unconcern.

"Hold his head up!" cries one women.

A man in a heavy woolen coat turns to a station worker and screams, "Get a doctor! Call the hospital." He offers his scarf as a temporary bandage.

A university student takes the scarf, while a woman tries to calm the old man and holds his head up. Others, who cannot help, gasp or shield their eyes, while another man sneers in distain at their sympathy.

"Be calm. Be calm. Help is coming. You're going to be alright," the woman assures him.

The Hassidim had made the mistake of ignoring the taunts and abuse of his tormentors. The wretched scene is becoming commonplace. A wave of nationalism has made many, who once considered themselves loyal Poles, struggling to justify their place in their own country – in their own home. A few years earlier, in the Polish-Soviet War, Jews fought for Polish independence with the Polish Legion under Józef Piłsudski. Although the largest minority, the sacrifice was not enough.

Jewish self-exclusion from Polish society stoked tensions as well. Despite co-existence over eight centuries, Jews who tried to build bridges between Jew and gentile were often scorned and exiled by their own people. The next generation of Poles and Jews, however, will have integration forced upon them by a shared holocaust. Three million Polish gentiles and three million Polish Jews will be murdered in concentration camps, prisons, streets, and battlefields. Tens of thousands of Christian Polish men, women, and children will lose their lives in attempts to rescue Polish Jews.

Poland had been independent for only three years by 1921. After more than a century of partitions by the Russian, German, Austro-Hungary empires, the country re-emerged ruined and ravaged. One third of the population is represented by non-Polish minorities. Its boundaries were limited to what Poles considered manageable, even though its defeat of Soviet forces in 1920 entitled it to more territory. Ahead, now, was the struggle to rebuild a nation upon a foundation of rubble, distrust, chaos, and myth.

The scene in the central rail station is another flashpoint in a newborn and turbulent land. A multitude of political parties with different ideologies and voter bases pull the people in disparate directions. As furor echoes within the train station, outside other perverse storms are gathering. Pogroms, assassinations, rampant corruption, foreign intrigues plague the newly formed state. Many are caught in the middle, not knowing that Poland's darkest days are still before it. The chaos is a blight and an opportunity. For some, it might be a midwife of noble causes; for others, a chance to cut deals.

Those who reason that their prospects to re-build are slipping away, find themselves looking an ocean away for hope. Europe had been giving up its children to America for hundreds of years. But, the once open door is closing. Following the First World War, the U.S. imposed harsh immigration quotas. Opportunity in The New Colossus for the "huddled masses" was fading. Emma Lazarus's "lamp beside the golden door" was growing dim. Yet, they keep coming. Communities splinter apart. Families separate. Hope is no more than a gambol. People make their bet on a strange country thousands of miles into the west.

Not far from the echoes of the horrid screams, laughter, excitement, and tears fill a comfortable apartment as adults embrace and children cling to their parents in innocent bewilderment. While the Hassidim is writhing in pain, a family gathering is taking place at a home in the Muranów neighborhood of the same central part of Warsaw. They have come together to wish *l'chaim* and bid farewell to members of the clan who are leaving for America. Although this family of four will be joining other family members there, they are leaving so much behind.

While the adults drift into small groups, four-year-old Abram Dzierzgowsky sits in a chair by a window overlooking his neighborhood. The streaming sunlight illuminates tiny particles of dust swirling like snowflakes. He watches with his grey-blue eyes and is fascinated. Abram dips his head into the squall to feel the warmth. He closes his eyes and smiles. He's found something new and it pleases him. Although only a toddler, the flame of his curiosity is inextinguishable, even rebellious. He wonders about other discoveries he'll find, if not today maybe tomorrow.

As Abram savors the wonderments of being a young boy and the simple adventures of discovery, grownups move in and out of groups in an adjacent room. Children lose their inhibitions and rush between adults playing games, feeding off one another's energy and excitement. The clamor sends two brothers to a semi-secluded corner away from the ruckus. They trade thoughts and share memories over drinks.

Within a short time, their banter is interrupted. A bright faced seven-year-old crashes into their conversation. Wide-eyed Berel Dzierzgowsky is eager to ask questions and understand all things. When he is not gazing intently at a new finding, he seems to have a perpetual smile on his face and in his voice. He is his father's pride. The incessant questions and unbridled curiosity are a cherishment lost with age. His father Jozef finds fondness for life through his son's enthusiasm for it.

Berel pulls on Jozef's pant leg: "Pappa, why do the adults say *l'chaim* every time they drink their wine?"

Jozef gently reminds his son that it is rude to interrupt, but then he softly beams and answers. "Well. 'to life' is a tribute to what God has given us. Our family, our health, our friends – the things that are worth living for." Josef pauses: "And to have them is to be grateful and humble."

Jozef strokes his son's small face. But Berel, unsatisfied, continues with his questions: "But what about the people who are sick, or do not have family? Lazar, the rag-seller lives alone. I never see him with friends or children. He has no wife. Does he say *l'chaim*, too?"

Jozef smiles sadly. Even if his son's questions seem ceaseless and, at times, challenging, Josef feels obliged to answer. Always asking, questioning, trying to understand. The more things defied an explanation, the more the questions. It was an early mark of a scholar.

"Lazar says *l'chaim*, too." Jozef assures his son. "Life is also hope. Without hope, there is very little life. *L'chaim* means there will be a tomorrow. And tomorrow means all is possible."

Satisfied with his response and eager to return to adult conversation, Joseph tells Berel: "Look there! Abram, Geiga, and Riva are having cake. Why don't you join them and let me know how good it tastes? Quick! Before it's all gone."

"Okay Pappa." Even at seven years old, Berel knows his constant questions could exasperate. He realizes it when adults change subjects or send him on an errand. Berel runs off to join his younger cousins.

Aron, Berel's uncle, smiles and says to his brother. "He never stops, does he? How do you keep up, Professor?"

"Barely," says the law school lecturer.

"I don't want to discourage him. But his questions often don't have answers. And I can't blame him for that, can I?"

Aron pours himself and Jozef a second drink. They lift their glasses with a grin.

"*L'chaim.*"

"You know, I was reading about this a while ago," starts Aron: "The origin of the expression *l'chaim*. One version has an interesting twist. According to a commentary on the old scriptures, it comes from ancient Jewish court records. In capital offenses, the verdict of life or death would be announced by the judges. *L'mitah* meant 'death.' *L'chaim* was 'life.' If the outcome was 'death,' the condemned would be offered a strong wine to ease the pain of execution."

"Mmmm. So, you are saying that perhaps *l'chaim* more accurately translates as 'for life,' not 'to life'?" asks the law professor.

"If you go by that version, I suppose … then, yes." Aron nods.

"I'll stay with the traditional one. It's less dark."

Jozef gulps down another mouthful of wine and confesses: "Although in these times, there is an uncomfortable truth about the ancient interpretation."

Aron dreamily gazes out the window and mutters: "We will live, and we will see."

"What?" Jozef reacts.

"*Pozhivom, povidem*…It's what our Russian friends like to say," Aron quotes.

Abram, Geiga, and Riva have already had their first round of sweet delicacies by the time Berel joins them at the dessert table. Geiga – Abram's older sister by two years – has taken command of the children's feast, pointing out which treats are recommended and who should sample what first. Riva – Abram and Geiga's cousin – is five years old and takes Geiga's commands eagerly. To Aron and Kara – her parents – her prettiness is their pride, just as Berel's budding intellect delights his parents.

Dzierzgowsky and its derivations were common surnames among Jews and Catholic Poles. Despite religious separation of Jews and gentiles, centuries of living beside one another resulted in many marriages of mixed bloodline. Particularly, common were members of Polish gentry seeking salvation from destitution by marrying into Jewish families of the middleclass. The result was a blended population segment. Many families didn't know whether they had mixed bloodlines. Riva was probably the fruit from such a family tree. She was fair and blue-eyed. Her blond hair curled finely around her little forehead and down her apple cheeks. When she smiled, her eyes lit up and her angelic tiny face could force a grin against the will of the hardest of hearts. Her father and mother have made her the center of their lives. They resist the urge to spoil her, but their resolve often wilts when put to the test.

As the day passes into night, guests gradually leave the party with final hugs and tearful kisses. The children strain to stay awake. The wide yawns from the little mouths are signals that the time has come. Life is moving on. There is a feeling of no return. Trunks are filled, passports secured, travel plans to the port confirmed. Excitement entwines with grief.

Aron sees his daughter's eyes are heavy. Before she falls asleep and has to be carried home, he picks her up and softly kisses her. "Riva. We have to go, it's time to say goodbye to Abram and Geiga."

"Yes, Poppa."

Aron sets her down. Riva runs to her cousins like a loyal puppy. Without being prompted, she holds little Abram and kisses him. The scene brings sad smiles and watery eyes. While Abram stands still, Riva turns to Geiga. The two toddlers embrace. Will this be the last time?

Dawid – Abram and Geiga's father – walks over to the children and lifts Riva. He, too, kisses her. He carries her to Aron's waiting arms.

"This is a part of us we will miss so much." Dawid tells Aron. "You must bring her back to us when you visit us in New York."

"Yes cousin. We will bring her," he assures. "And, we will write, of course."

"When you do, don't forget; Dzierzgowski is spelled with a "J" in English."

"Of course…my American cousin" smiles Aron.

Jozef moves in beside Dawid to place his hand on his shoulder.

"And Jozef," Dawid turns and demands, "You let us know as soon as Berel enters university. That should be in a year or so."

"Don't worry. Our little professor will not disappoint."

"We will say a *Berakah* in his name," says Dawid.

"Don't forget his teachers, God help them." Aron suggests. All three welcome a laugh to ease the tension.

After a moment of silence and an exchange of weary smiles, Aron says: "Keep well Dawid. We will keep you, Chaya, and the children deep in our hearts."

"Yes, and your parents and brothers in America," adds Jozef.

The words mask the unspoken questions: "Will we ever see each other again? And, if so, under what circumstances?"

The night comes. Dawid, Chaya, Geiga, and Abram are alone in the apartment. The past is over. Tomorrow, they begin their journey. Tomorrow, they let go of the sorrow and part with any thoughts of regret.

3. Steerage

Yevheniy Demchenko woke and breathed the foul air in the steerage hold of the *D.D. Rotterdam*. For five days, he and his fellow passengers have endured prison-like conditions as they make the journey across the Atlantic from Copenhagen. The stench of unattended vomit, filthy bodies, and the nearby toilets engulfed the senses. A noxious miasma, thick enough to penetrate clothing and even flesh, makes the trip a nightmarish ordeal. Yet Yevheniy, like the millions of others who over the years withstood the journey, irresistibly heeds the call of a promise that justifies all the misery.

Yevheniy leaps from his upper berth to the deck. He slept in his clothes as he does every night. He puts on his padded jacket, grabs his old fiddler's hat, and scurries past the row of bunks and the rank odors. Once past the ship's machinery, he is topside. It is early and most of the passengers are still asleep. But the sixteen-year-old from western Ukraine can't control his restlessness. Every morning he gets up before sunrise, runs to the top deck and slings his arms over the ship's rails to survey the horizon. There, waiting for the sun to rise, he can smell the fresh air, take in the calm, and awe at the vastness of the ocean seascape. The top deck was not only a relief from the wretched and chaotic conditions below, but also the environment for serious daydreaming. He is weary and dirty, but youthful and exhilarated. An internal hunger feeds his imagination, stokes his dreams.

The hunger for his new life in America nearly matches the hunger gnawing in his stomach. The food in steerage is repellent, and the constant motion makes consumption unthinkable. Throughout the long grueling march from his Ukrainian village outside Lviv, Yevheniy leaned on his grandfather's words for sustenance: "A hungry wolf is stronger than a satisfied dog."

"That's me...a strong wolf," Yevheniy assures himself as he prays. "I will be an American. I will work hard and try to be pious." He makes the sign of the cross and then runs his hand down the features of his broad olive-toned face to wipe away the mist. His greenish eyes flash under a severe brow. His tatty hat covers a crop of light hair that curls over his ears.

The crew told the passengers that by this time tomorrow, they would have their first glimpse of the Statue of Liberty. At last! The symbol of the future…the symbol of the big, powerful country – his future, his country!

As he dreams of that future, an older man moves quietly nearby, a few feet from Yevheniy at the railing. His slender frame casts a silhouette against the misty dawn. His eyes are intense, but his mien is effortlessly amicable and polite.

The Ukrainian acknowledges his new companion with a nod and a smile.

"How do you do," says the man in Polish, as he turns and acknowledges Yevheniy's innocent, obvious enthusiasm.

"Well sir …and you?" says Yevheniy.

Their overlapping dialects allow them to carry a conversation.

Yevheniy does not recognize the man from steerage. His fine overcoat suggests that he is probably from, at least, the second-class compartments. His manner is respectful and his eyes seem kind.

The stranger takes off his glove and extends his hand.

"Dawid Dzierzgowsky," he says

"Yevheniy Demchenko. But my friends call me Genko."

"Well, Pan Demchenko, it's a pleasure to meet you. We will be in America by tomorrow they say. Are you excited?"

"Oh, yes Pan Dzierzgowsky. It's been a long trip, but I try to make good use of it."

Dawid detects Yevheniy's eagerness to talk, so he urges him on: "What have you been doing 'to make good use' of all this time, then?"

"I practice my English, of course. I also know some of the questions I will be asked. America doesn't like criminals or men with more than one wife, that's a polygamist. I've also never been in prison or sent to a sanatorium. I have more than $25 in my pocket – so I'm in fine shape," Yevheniy says proudly.

Dawid smiles and nods with a glint of a man who is impressed. He continues the questioning: "Have you been travelling alone all this time, Yevheniy?"

"Yes, but my brother Olek will be meeting me. He's been in America for almost two years working for a milling company. He sent me my ticket a month ago. Maybe my mother and poppa will be coming, we hope."

"My brothers and my father will be meeting us too," says Dawid. "Will you be working with your brother?"

"Oh, at first …maybe for a year. After that I will be old enough to join the United States Marine Corps. They are the best fighting men in America."

Before Dawid has a chance to ask any further questions, Yevheniy pulls a folded sheet of paper from the inside pocket of his jacket. He unfolds it carefully and shows it to Dawid. "Olek sent it to me."

Dawid looks at a recruitment advertisement ripped from a magazine. The illustration portrays a uniformed military man with a blade-like physique. Brass buttons and red and gold chevrons adorn his navy dress tunic. Rifle slung over his shoulder, he marches resolutely with head held high and slightly turned toward the reader as if saying: "Join me!".

"Well," Dawid reacts, as he refolds the ad and returns to Yevheniy: "It sounds like you've made some serious plans"

"Oh yes," Yevheniy assures him. "As soon as I get off this ship I am going to change my name. I have a new country. I will need a new name … a real American name."

"What do you mean, 'as soon you get off this ship'? Don't you need to go through processing first?"

"Oh no, I'm not waiting at all. Olek wrote and said he knew a man from Ireland who didn't want to keep his Irish name. He made the officials change his name on his entry documents…right at Ellis Island. His name is Halloran."

"Mmm," mutters Dawid. "And what did he change it to?"

"No, no. That is his name! It used to be O'Halloran."

"I see," says Dawid, trying to keep a serious face. "Well, my little boy and girl are Abram and Geiga. I think we will be changing their names to something sounding more American, also."

"Oh, I definitely will be changing both my names! I've had a lot of time to think about it, and I finally decided what I want for my American name. A new life, a new country, no old names!"

"And you will become …?" Dawid begins, leaving Yevheniy to fill in the blank.

"Gene – no more Yevheniy!"

"Very good...Gene. And what about your new American surname?"

"Dembrowski, GENE Dembrowski," Yevheniy announces with the ardor of a conquistador planting his flag.

A broad smile spreads across Dawid's face and his eyes twinkle. He clasps his hands behind his back and tilts his head in respect. Then, standing at attention, he says: "Well, Corporal Gene Dembrowski, I think you will make an excellent U.S. Marine."

Yevheniy beams and nods in agreement.

"And you, Sir? Will you be changing your name?" Yevheniy asks.

"Well, in a way. My mother and father came to New York fifteen years ago. We will take their surname – Jergowsky, Jer-GOW-skee. We are not Americanizing the name, just Americanizing the spelling."

"Jer-GOW-skee," repeats Yevheniy.

Dawid smiles and suggests: "What say I buy us something from the ship's commissary. A little celebration of our new destinies as fellow-Americans," suggests Dawid.

Yevheniy's face bursts with the brightness of July Fourth fireworks. It would be the first time he's had decent food in more than two weeks. The meals onboard were barely edible and at the emigrant hotels near the embarkation docks they were not that much better. He nods enthusiastically. Dawid puts his hand on Gene's shoulder and ushers him in the direction of the commissary for second class passengers. As they move away from the railing, Dawid takes a last look at the endless sea.

"Are these mad delusions? So many dreamers...Can this country really accommodate all their dreams? If America can do that, indeed, anything is possible," he says to himself.

"As Aron likes to say: *Pozhivom, povidem*: We shall live, and we shall see."

4. Warsaw, 1944

An SS soldier from the *Sturmbrigade* sits on a pile of rubble in what's left of Warsaw. He might as well be sitting atop human skulls. His unit is made up of mostly former criminals, cashiered rejects from other units, and officially-categorized "sadistic morons." All are considered disposable. In exchange for their service, they are allowed to commit any crime. He and his men have murdered, tortured, raped, and looted their way through the war. During the Warsaw uprising, they reportedly murdered 500 children in daycare with bayonets and rifle butts so as to not to waste ammunition. The commander of this herd is Oskar Dirlewanger. He is known among the Wehrmacht as "the butcher." A convicted child molester himself, he not only condones such outrages, he orders them.

The boney features of the soldier's face form a buffoonish portrait when he grins. He draws a puff from his cigarette with an air of self-satisfaction. The war has given him power he never knew in civilized society. What this master of the universe does not know is that his head is in the crosshairs of a sniper from the *Armia Krajowa* – the Polish Home Army. Given his heinous life, his final reckoning seems too swift. Like many of the heroes of this war, this criminal's name will be forgotten.

Berel Dzierzgowsky steadies the barrel of his rifle and breathes softly as his finger caresses the trigger. The once brilliant chemical engineer is a veteran street fighter.

His father, Jozef, and uncles were consumed early in the Nazi occupation. Intellectuals were the immediate target: a late-night knock at the door, transport to Pawiak prison, and summary execution. Berel's mother died of grief; his wife was swept away in a random roundup. Their parting was as abrupt as it was unimaginable. The end came as simply as leaving home one morning and returning later – never to see her again.

Thus far, he's been able to survive through his knowledge of the city, his instincts, and the assistance of righteous Poles. A year earlier, his professional skills were put to use during the Jewish uprising: making explosives, fire bottles, pipe bombs, and grenades. They were produced by the thousands. An early specialty was a grenade built inside a short segment of water pipe. It was easily concealed inside a shirt sleeve or under a trouser leg, and exploded when any forceful contact activated the detonation cap.

For several weeks between April and May of 1943, the ghetto smoldered and gasped on the smell of decaying and burnt flesh. Berel escaped to the Aryan side through fetid sewers, helped by contacts in the *Zegota* (the Polish Jewish underground). He lurked and scavenged the sewers like a brutal animal.

Cut off and under fire, the city's sewer system was the only operational means of travel for the resistance. Berel slogged his way through excrement, corpses, and debris. The sludge was knee deep in some places, and in others up to a man's waist. The only gasp of relatively fresh air was below the open manholes. Men and women filled their lungs with air from the city's fumy streets and moved on as far as their aching legs and backs could carry them. Only in the main tunnels could they stand erect.

The stench and darkness drove many insane. Berel struggled to keep his own sanity as he dragged himself through a cavum of waste and rot. He heard the moans and screams of those who had lost their way. He waded past corpses of the many who had drown or been killed by explosives dropped from above.

When he emerged, he was a mumbling shell of his former self, yet immediately connected with the revived Jewish Fighting Organization—*Żydowska Organizacja Bojowa* (ŻOB). Eventually he joined the *Armia Krajowa*. In the Home Army's underground workshops Berel developed submachine guns, mortars, and flame throwers. His code-name became "Blaze." Arms-making did not assuage his anger, however. He sought clarity at the frontline – in the streets and rubble of Warsaw. He needed to see the face of his enemy. He wanted to make it personal.

While Berel focuses through the scope, he hears his spotter, Andrzej:

"What's the little pigeon doing now?"

"Yapping …and grinning like a clown," snorts Berel.

"Is the shot clear?" asks Andrzej.

"Crystal," answers Berel.

"*Kurwa*," Andrzej smirks.

Berel pulls the trigger, the rifle cracks, and the German's head explodes – all in an instant. As the body lies twitching and spouting blood, the other *Sturmbrigaders* scramble for cover or begin shooting. The tilt of their comrade's fall gives away the general direction of the shot, but they can't see their targets. Gradually, they attempt to close in.

Berel and Andrzej fire back, forcing the Germans to take cover.

"We need to get out of here. How's Fritz?" asks Berel.

"He is well."

When Dirlewanger's men reach the sniper roost, the Poles are gone. All that's left are a few spent shells and a dead *landser*. The Germans pull over their comrade to see if they recognize him. As they lift the remains, a grenade explodes and fills their bodies with shrapnel.

Berel and Andrzej know the labyrinthine path to the command post like the back of their hand. As in Stalingrad, the ruins of Warsaw offer excellent cover for both sides. Since the beginning of the uprising, the city has become a network of barricades and shelters. Citizens fortify their positions with concrete slabs, sand, and iron rods, hammered into the earth.

Not all of the killing involves street fighting or hand-to-hand combat. When the Germans get frustrated, they hammer the forts with the colossal *Mörser Karl* siege mortar, also, known as "Thor." Six of these monsters were built for use on the Eastern Front. Now three are deployed against Warsaw. Each mortar fires shells that weigh up to 5,000 pounds to a range of more than 10 kilometers (6 miles). The blasts tear off the roofs and upper floors of buildings. People and walls are thrown about as if they were hit by a cyclone. "Throwers" is the name the Poles give the mortars.

The *Mörser Karl* levels neighborhoods. Residents are entombed alive or killed by concussion. For several minutes after the explosion, the semi-conscious survivors are pelted with human organs, limbs, spinal cords. It was said: "If you squeezed a handful of Warsaw soil, blood would run out."

When they reach the command bunker, Berel and Andrzej share a ration of water. The heat of August mixes with the fumes of the seething city. Berel wipes the sweat from his dark, deep-set eyes. In his university days, those eyes were bright with curiosity and anticipation. Today, the future is gone. He has lost everything and everyone. Berel Dzierzgowsky goes by a code name. The people from his youth would not recognize him. His once lush dark hair is thin and grey. The creases in his face are deep. His body is scarred. But his mind is sharp and his muscles are taut. His emotions are worn but raw with hate for the occupiers.

As Berel and Andrzej sip from the canteen, they nod to one another: "*L'chaim,*" toasts Berel.

"*Na Zdrowie!*" replies Andrzej.

"Listen up!…Meeting…Now!" announces Stepan, the local commander. Stepan Krol is in his mid-twenties – tall, blonde, an experienced soldier. Half his face is gruesomely scarred – the result of a German grenade that tore off his left cheek. A Home Army nurse stitched it back on with suture thread and sewing needles.

The men and women at the command post quickly huddle around their captain. They know the battle for Warsaw is about to intensify. The Home Army was supposed to hold the Germans for only a week. The Soviet army on the other side of the Vistula River was expected to sweep the Germans out of Warsaw. Almost a month later, the Soviets remain motionless while the city burns. The Polish arsenal, medical supplies, and food rations are running out. Ammunition will last another four days. The Home Army does not accept volunteers. What would be the point when there are no weapons to arm them or resources to train them? The Western Allies have dropped supplies, but only one-third gets through. The rest is recovered by the Wehrmacht. For the men and women who refuse to give up, it will become simply a matter of how one chooses to die.

"We have a new objective," says the commander. "Gdansk Train Station."

An emotional tide surges through the room. People look about and grimly nod. These orders had to come. The train station is a vital northern link. It separates the Home Army troops in the Old Town from the reinforcements. The German garrison will greet the attackers with machine gun fire and tank shells. Their defenses include an armored train. Only one in ten Poles is fully armed.

As much as the station is a military target, it is also a symbol of human atrocity. The Nazis used the western part of the station as a collection point for transport to the Treblinka extermination camp. Almost 300,000 Jews and other "undesirables" were herded from the ghetto. The *Umschlagplatz*, as the Germans called it, processed as many as ten thousand a day. It was likely Rebecca Dzierzgowska's last memory of her city, unless she was executed on a whim of the SS before reaching the deportation center.

Berel and Rebecca met at university, seemingly in another lifetime. On one frigid day, in the teeth of a biting wind, Berel thought he had seen the most beautiful girl in Warsaw. He fixated on her as she walked the cobbled street through the main gate. Her strides were defiant, her bearing indomitable against the aching cold. In her wake trailed her plush black hair and a long crimson scarf. A leather bag slung over her shoulder and her arms were folded beneath her breasts.

She moved gracefully by. He was too stunned to muster the nerve to approach. The worst thing would have been to stop her but stand inert with nothing to say. The humiliation would have been crushing.

Berel had been a devoted researcher for too long. The regimen of scholarship left a stifling cover of rust over his social skills. His spontaneity was manqué due to an obsession with theoretical purity. Idiosyncratic minds perform well under laboratory conditions but not necessarily in the wild.

In academia, every question has three possible responses: "yes," "no," and "perhaps." This was a welcome liberation from real world complexity. But in the real world all he could do was gawk helplessly as this wondrous discovery vanished, perhaps forever, he thought.

In his cluttered bachelor apartment, he could not get Rebecca out of his head. He needed to memorialize the sight rather than let it fade gradually from his mind. Rather than prepare for lecture, he scratched out a poem in his best hand.

> Across the city square she strode,
>
> Reigning over the ground she set foot,
>
> I watched the young queen disappear,
>
> And I too moved on,
>
> To face a life without her.

"Not bad for an engineer," he thinks. He sighs, folds the paper in an envelope, then puts it in a bottom drawer.

"No point in leaving your emotions out for people to see," he reasons, and then consoles: "A little bit of heartache is good for the soul." He leans back in his desk chair, places his hands behind his head and dreams of things that might have been.

A few days later, a Chopin concert hosted by the university at Holy Cross Church attracted students, faculty, and lovers of the master's music. It's an excellent diversion from Berel's newfound loneliness. As he walks up to a desk to grab a program, a delicate female voice from behind asks: "Could you get a program for me as well, sir?" Berel takes a second pamphlet, turns and...There she is! His queen is now face-to-face with him.

She's even more exquisite up close. Her beauty is jolting. Her raven hair frames the ivory glow of her gentle face. Her fawn-like brown eyes are magnetic, dazzling, and intelligent. When she smiles, he feels special, but at the same time humbled, undeserving, and, unfortunately, speechless.

Through his shock, he hears himself say: "Oh my God...!"

Rebecca looks back at him confused. She tilts her head like a curious French poodle and asks: "Do I know you?"

He blushes and is stricken with terror at being forced to talk to the woman he has already placed on a pedestal. His head is completely empty. He's too consumed by the thought that this could be his only chance. "I'll either be a pathetic ass or maybe the happiest man in the world. Damn, think of something to say, you moron!"

He finally stutters like an eight-year-old trying to explain to his parents a bad report card. "Ah, errrr...No, no, ah...you don't."

Her Majesty grins and her eyes light up even more. They both know he's in trouble. In full command now, she waits for what he might say next.

There is some silence, and then he tries again.

"I saw you going through the university's gate two days ago." A guilty smile stretches across his reddened face like an adolescent caught in the act of staring at an older girl.

Still silent, Rebecca waits for further signs of intelligent life.

"And I just watched you. That's it, I just watched you. And I...ah

...didn't expect to see you again." He nods like there is some finality to his words; as if at the same time he's thinking: "I'm done. I lost my chance. I hope I made you laugh. Nice to have met you."

"You just watched me?" she repeats, making him feel even more stupid.

All he can do is shrug and admit: "Ah ...yeah."

There is no witty follow up. His concentration has gone. It would not return until he is on his way home. By then, the clever comebacks would flow forth. For now, sadly, his mind is swooning, and his mouth is babbling.

Fortunately for him, Rebecca decides to put an end to his misery. As a young woman, Rebecca became aware of her allure early. But she struggled with it. The attention clashed with her shyness. Her grandmother, however, warned her that pretty girls do not have the luxury of being shy. Withdrawal signals aloofness and snobbery. "You will hurt people's feelings, dear, if you don't learn to recognize kindness and respond," said her Bobe. Rebecca's modesty inhibited her instinct to please, sometimes producing silly moments.

Rebecca struggled to trust the attention she attracted. Nevertheless, she couldn't help being intrigued by this graceless young man. He may be incoherent, but he somehow speaks honestly. She finds herself paying more attention to his eyes. Besides, how much longer could this quivering speech go on?

"Could this girl actually be unaware of how beautiful she is?" Berel asks himself.

"Could this boy really be as shy and awkward as I am?" Rebecca wonders.

"Thank you for the program," she says taking it from his hand.

The pamphlet glides through his fingers, but his hand doesn't move. His eyes focus on hers.

Rebecca stands still, waiting for an invitation to sit with him at the concert.

The tension builds. Berel finally asks: "May I sit with you? That is, if you are not already with someone." He breathes silently. "There, I did it."

"Please do. I often come to concerts by myself. It will be good to have some company." She finishes with an inadvertent wink.

They smile at one another with joy and relief.

From that day, they were a couple. Soon, they were finishing each other's words and knowing each other's thoughts. They were married a year later, and believed they would live happily forever.

Berel and Rebecca were the couple everyone wanted to be around. Smiling, caring, fun, and self-effacing, they attracted friends easily. He, the brilliant scientist who carried himself breezily and bore his brilliance quietly. And, she, his loving partner. The music from the concert where they met would play on – no matter what!

"When?" comes a voice from the back of the bunker.

"The 20th," says Stepan. "In two days. We're going in with a force of about 1,000. We'll have night cover."

"What are we bringing to the party?" asks another voice.

"Whatever we can scrape together. The army is stretched," says Stepan. "Blaze! What's the situation with grenades?"

"We will have them," assures Berel. "There was another unexploded shell found last week. A group of scouts and kids recovered plenty of material."

Andrzej nudges the man next to him. "God bless the Czechs. That's where the munition plants are. They're good at producing duds."

"Good," nods Stepan. "I'll let everyone know more about the plans as soon as I learn them."

5. Gdansk Train Station

The train station is littered with corpses, hanging from burnt out vehicles, and scattered over the ground like animal hides. Warsaw burns in delirium. The streets are covered with a reddish grey film – the residue of burnt bricks. Flames howl. Beams of buildings groan before collapsing. From this fever-born world a blistering moon hangs in the grainy night smog.

It's the third day of the assault – August 22nd. The first night's fighting reduced the Polish ranks by 100. On the second night, they lost 300. Still, the attackers pressed on. A group of women sappers were able to put charges at the entrance of a building. When the doors blew apart, the men rushed in and cut down the defenders. Despite the overwhelming odds, the Poles learned the Germans had received as good as they delivered. Their position was littered with rotting bodies. A recovered diary recorded that several Wehrmacht and Ukrainian auxiliaries had committed suicide while addled with fear and exhaustion. But this was an isolated victory.

At another German-held building near a train platform, an SS trooper stoops to examine a wounded starling struggling to hold on to life. "Mother in heaven," he says to himself. He gently lifts the bird with one of his claws and grabs his canteen to share some droplets of precious water.

Two weeks earlier this dispenser of life and death was taking part in the massacre at the Wola district. He and his comrades went from house to house shooting inhabitants. Many were shot on the spot, some were killed after torture and sexual assault. Victims included women, children, the elderly, and patients at local hospitals. Bodies of dead and wounded were thrown on pyres. He assisted in rounding up civilians to be used as human shields when approaching resistance positions. One of his individual contributions to the war effort was the murder of a young mother who refused to be separated from her daughter. In a state of pique, he then shot the five-year-old as well. Now this petty monster's only concern is for the life of a common creature.

As he strokes the starling he hears a crack. A bullet pierces his neck. His last thought: "I am dead."

Andrzej Sobczak lowers his rifle and squats down behind the barricade where he has been tracking movements along the German held defense. "One less pigeon fancier?" asks Berel.

Andrzej nods.

"We should get out of here. They will be zeroing in on us."

"You can. I want to recover as much material as I can before we retreat for good."

Sobczak's face is drained of any signs of emotion. Without looking up at Berel, he speaks. "Last week my sister's neighborhood was hit by a thrower. Her building held, but her ten-year-old son was out in the courtyard. All she found of him was his leg. It was still in his shoe."

Andrzej lifts his head: "Do Jews believe in the afterlife?"

"It depends on the Jew."

"What does your testament say?"

"It says 'that man will receive his just reward.' I'm a scientist. All I know is: matter and energy can't be created or destroyed. It only changes form. That's the closest I come to a belief in an eternal soul."

Suddenly, an explosion. A mortar shell has landed.

"We gotta get out of here! ... Now!" yells Berel. He turns to see Andrzej's body slumped against the blood-splattered wall. He grabs the rifle they had been sharing, takes a final glimpse at his friend, and leaps from the hiding place to seek out the nearest bunker. When he arrives, he joins three men and one woman: "Are we all that's left?"

"It's over. We are withdrawing," says a tall man in a Wehrmacht field jacket and helmet.

"Any news about the front? The Russians?"

"The front is moving. But not the Russians. They're still on the other side of the Vistula. Meanwhile, French cities are being liberated. So is Belgium. Poland is on its own – as we have been since the beginning."

"The airdrops?"

"Most aren't getting through. The pilots are all volunteers – mostly Poles. I helped recover two of them. I don't know if they made it. They were badly hurt."

Berel nods, knowingly. It's just a matter of time and place.

He decides to remain behind to collect unspent ammunition and abandoned weapons. Eventually he separates from the group and operates on his own. After an hour, he hears the sounds of jack-boots getting louder. They are closing in.

"I should have gotten away earlier. Now I'm fucked,"

The way back to safety is through the marshalling yards. But to get there he must cross the open area in front of the main building. He has no choice. He's weary, but he won't leave the ammunition behind to lighten his load. The assault force has fought too dearly for it.

He moves cautiously at first and tries to avoid the lights. He must make a break across a semi-lit train yard or wait for them to come for him. Berel takes a deep breath and hikes the ammo belts on his shoulders. He makes a headlong dash in the open. As he crosses the collection area he hears shouting. He's been spotted. Bullets ping off the stone surface on either side. He can feel the fragments at his feet. He makes a run across the station plaza to the marshalling yard. Leaping over the tracks while carrying the extra ammo forces him to break stride. Fighting for three days without adequate food, water, and rest has brought him to the brink of madness.

Suddenly, he feels metal pass through his body. Berel falls and writhes in shock and pain. Blood soaks his clothes and flows from his mouth. He crawls over the track rails, grasping for every moment of life left. He stops. He can feel his heart pumping the blood from his body. In a few minutes, he will be dead – but his senses refuse to die. In his last conscious moments, groaning in his own blood, he tries to calm himself with final thoughts of Rebecca. At last, he goes still.

Three figures walk toward his body. They are hoping he is still alive. Perhaps there will be enough life in him for a little sport. Torturing Poles and Jews while they are dying puts a self-congratu-latory touch to a kill. One of the men bends down and grabs Berel's shoulder by his shirt. He yanks him over on his back.

Somewhere on the precipice of death, Berel Dzierzgowsky finds the might to pull a pipe grenade out from his sleeve. In one final act, he slams it to the ground. The blast kills the closest man instantly. The other two race around like human torches in the darkness. Their final screams echo through the gloom of train yards as they squeal for mercy. The last audible word from this scorched corner of the

Gdansk Train Station is *Mati*! – the Ukrainian word for mother.

Strewn across the tracks are the twisted, charred corpses of four men. Their remains will be tagged as "unknown." Thus is the pageantry of war.

One *Armia Krajowa* survivor offered a more storied account: "When you fight for your freedom you get a very special feeling that never comes again. One doesn't worry about getting wounded or dying…It was not a feeling of revenge either. We did not feel hatred, just exhilaration in fighting for freedom."

Several generations later, many years after the last Soviet soldier leaves Polish soil, a memorial is placed at the site of the train station. It symbolizes a mass grave beside a stone statue of a grieving mother. A single rough-hewn plaque serves as an anonymous and emblematic headstone.

> In honor of the heroic
>
> soldiers of the Home Army
>
> insurgent troops…fallen in the attack
>
> on the Gdansk Station
>
> between 20th and 22nd August 1944.

There are no names.

Freedom came to Berel that night. Aside from fighting for freedom, the reward for this once gifted and sacrificial life is – as it was with Abraham: "to return to rest with his fathers." What life he and his beloved Rebecca would have lived, will never be fulfilled. They leave behind no legacies. There was no one to say *kaddish* over Berel's body. And no one left alive to grieve.

6. Hürtgen Forest, 1944

At the battalion aid station, an army surgeon growls at his crew. Through clenched teeth he roars: "Let him die in the fucking snow. Did ya hear me! Get this piece of shit out of here!"

The surgeon's assistant and the aid man look at each other and nod. They begin gathering up the German and bags of plasma. As they near the door their commander shouts: "They started this. He's to blame too." With this last flourish, the doctor slumps down on a stool and hangs his head in exhaustion.

Without a word, the lieutenant and his sergeant move the boy in the direction of a second tent. Away from the cold and the rants of their captain they set the wounded German down and continue giving him plasma. The soldier's body is rattling. He's talking hysterically. In between the gasps and bloody coughs, he yells out German names. The soldier was brought in that morning. Usually, wounded *Wehrmacht* don't survive on the battlefield unless recovered by their own medics. But because of his youth and the humanity of two reconnaissance litter bearers, he was brought to the battalion field clinic.

"Any idea what's this guy is saying lieutenant?" asks the sergeant as he prepares the syringes.

"He's calling someone named Max. It sounds like it might be his son."

"A son! He doesn't look old enough to have a girlfriend. Just another kid. Another fucking kid." The sergeant curses.

"We have 'em, too," his lieutenant reminds him.

The sergeant shakes his head in disgust.

The soldier is now speaking frantically. The lieutenant keeps translating.

"He keeps saying 'I love you Max. I will always be your father.'"

With what's left of his failing energy the soldier heaves a last outburst.

"I never wanted to leave you, please forgive me," translates the officer, who keeps his focus on the man's wounds.

The Americans keep administering the plasma. But they know from their training and experience this soldier's time is running out. He is no more than 17 or 18 years old. He is fair, baby-faced, blue-eyed, and in shock. In between his calls for his son he cries out an unfamiliar word – "*Sanitäter*!"

"What's that mean?"

"I don't know. Is there more plasma? These bags are freezing up."

"It's all I could carry."

"We're losing him," says the officer without changing expression or looking up.

The wounded man's eyes are starting to glaze. He is turning white and starting to convulse. Lieutenant Al Jergowsky looks down at the dying man. The German is looking back, but not at the American. He's looking past him…at something beyond this world. Finally, he takes one deep gasp. The medics look on helplessly and know what to expect. As he slips into oblivion he softly murmurs his last word: "*Mama*."

Both medical corpsmen have heard "Momma," "Mother," "Mom," "Mommy," in the last breaths of their own men before they let go.

Jergowsky and his sergeant, Francis Murphy, collapse into a heap. There is nothing but silence except for the whirling wind on the other side of the canvas tent. As they begin straightening up, they collect the half-empty bags of plasma and field instruments. Jergowsky looks down at the dead soldier and runs his hand over his face to close his eyes.

"I'll see you back at the command post, lieutenant," says Murphy.

"Oh. Murph?"

Frank Murphy turns to acknowledge.

"Try to get some rest."

Jergowsky grabs his gear and leaves the corpse where it lays. He walks out in the freezing cold. It's late December and Hitler's Ardennes counteroffensive has stalled. Meanwhile, the battle of Hürtgen Forest has raged since September. As the 1st and 3rd Armies take on the enemy from three sides, the 78th Division counterattacks to narrow the salient and drive through the German defenses.

Many of the men along Germany's Westwall are still wearing fatigues from the summer campaign. Hot showers and dry clothing are distant memories. No one expected the Germans would have this much fight left. But they are battling on German sacred soil. It will be the Western Front's counterpart to Stalingrad. The American replacement rates will be so high, the term 'combat veteran' will refer to anyone who survives the first day. By the end of the conflict, Hitler's last desperate gamble will involve more than a million men.

Lieutenant Jergowsky walks back to the main op tent. The battalion physician who ordered him out is now sitting on a trunk drinking from a tin cup of liberated cognac. He sees his deputy and says: "Do you think I'm a monster, Al?"

"No more than the rest of us, Greg."

"You know we lost Miller and Barrowcliff yesterday."

Al clenches his teeth.

Captain Greg Towne continues. "They were out looking for wounded. We found their jeep in the sector by the hill they call the crucifix. It was turned over and still running when a patrol got to it. Bill and Mel's bodies were strewn beside the wreck. Their heads were taken off."

Jergowsky looks at his commander with incomprehensible horror. But before he has time to react, Towne goes on.

"The Bosch string piano wire between the trees. We now have to weld metal blades on the jeeps as hood ornaments." He breathes deeply and says: "How do I write the letters to their families?" Towne takes another gulp from his tin. "All my life, I just wanted to be a doctor. I wanted to be a 'healer'," he says sarcastically as he stares at the frozen dirt floor. "Now I think sometimes, I would rather kill. What does it mean?"

Al gathers himself after what he's just heard about Miller and Barrowcliff and says. "It means you're human, I'm afraid."

The surgeon smirks and replies: "Then, what the hell does it mean to be human?"

After a silence, the lieutenant answers: "To err."

"I'll see you tomorrow, unless I see you later tonight.".

Towne nods and returns to his cognac.

*****

Eddie Todd patrols an unsecured area along the front. Every muscle in his body is knotted. Only his heart seems unbound as it thuds deep within his chest. He has been in action for only several weeks.

Not long ago he was enjoying a sensible and boring existence in rural Pennsylvania. Each day was predictable. Surroundings and faces were familiar. The peacefulness and calm were granted. But now, war has taken over his life. This is his world. There is danger with every footstep, and the silence is frightful. When the sounds of war subside, the loudest noise is his hammering heartbeat. He scans the terrain for anything distrustful, but eyes and ears can play tricks. He's unloaded several rounds today in the direction of a scampering rabbit and at the snap of a snow-laden tree branch.

He unknowingly approaches a foxhole when two arms appear reaching up from the earth. They hold a helmet. The "steel pot" is full of urine. Eddie looks on as the arms dump the contents and return to the underground. The scene is so weirdly jolting, he will never be able to erase it from his head. Todd gasps. "Shit! What in hell kind of place is this?" He moves on.

Every encounter conjures the feelings of a deranged and alienated world. "Insanity" captures the foulness, fears and anger of this place in a single word. War is a detachment from anything normal or natural. Where else can things be so horrid, absurd and bazaar? In the future, if anyone asks Eddie Todd "What was war like?" for some vague reason, of all his battlefield memories, the image of these two bodiless arms, reaching out of a hole clasping a helmet of waste will be the thought that first comes to mind. This is the Hürtgen and his baptism into the misery.

As he makes his way across this pitiless land, every tangled mass of undergrowth and logs are a potential machine gun nest. Every clump of brush is suspicious. Under the snow are trip wires that set off charges of TNT. Pillboxes are built into the sides of hills and camouflaged. The strongpoints, mortar positions, and mutually supporting weapons organize to form interlocking bands of fire.

Weeks of constant artillery attacks transform the landscape into a forest of shredded treetops – as if a giant scythe has swept through. Yellow-grey tree trunks and abandoned equipment clutter the ground. Human limbs and clothing hang from branches.

Forward artillery observers, engineers, and medics accompany advancing troops. Everyone suffers the same wretchedness. At night, men burrow themselves in foxholes and dugouts. In the dark, you can't tell if the stirrings above are your own men or the enemy's. Both sides are living under the same accursed conditions. Many are shot in the back as they unknowingly walk through or over an enemy position.

Through the morning gossamer glow, Todd can see the silhouettes of dispersed squads roaming a snowy landscape. Like him, the shadowy figures slog through drifting snow, fighting the biting cold, and suppressing the fear clutching at their hearts.

The worst fear is tree bursts. A single shell can scatter shards of fiery metal and pine over a fifty-yard area. The impulse is to fall to the earth but that only exposes more of your body. The best chance for survival is to stand upright, clinch your teeth and pray.

Suddenly, the Germans zero-in on the area where Todd is patrolling. Like the gust of a rolling storm, the artillery barrage sweeps through the American positions. Some of the men in his patrol huddle in makeshift foxholes, while others stand erect and motionless. The bombardment seems to last an eternity. Deadly debris swirls in a whirlwind of hot steel and jagged spikes of timber. All Todd can do is wait. Maybe this time he'll will be lucky, again.

Once the roar of the cannons quiets, the echo of screams and moans rumble through the woods. A chorus of groans, cries, pleas for help, and prayers writhes above the slaughter. The macabre din, the odor of exploding shells, and the smell of death hangs over the dead and the survivors.

Back at the battalion aid station, the men have a few hours of rest. The last troop of casualties have been treated and dispatched. Now is the time for regrouping before the next onslaught. Some men try to sleep. Others read their mail. And some just lie in their cots, close their eyes, and try to keep their minds blank.

Al Jergowsky seeks out his patch of earth in tent adjacent to the main op tent. The wind is fierce. There doesn't seem any way to warm up. The oil drum in the center of the tent is a converted furnace. It's blowing out heat, but even hugging it won't stop the shivering. He has already tried. Only a few weeks earlier it wasn't the cold and snow that made life unbearable. It was the relentless rain, sleet, and the mud. Men slept in foxholes and awoke in pools of water. Sometimes your legs were encased in ice and needed help from your buddies to break free. You never dried out. Now, a record winter has come to Europe. The suffering has entered a new phase. In the backdrop, howitzers grumble. When the mines go off and mortars land, the earth vomits up black soil and snow.

On his ground cover, Al takes off his boots and slips his legs under his sleeping bag. He's drained…but despite his depletion, doesn't know how much sleep he's actually going to get this night. You only half sleep at the front. No man sleeps well here. Although the darkness is profound, indistinct noises and ambiguous movements have a sinister feel. The tension of combat amplifies them.

Sometimes the best rest you get is when you let the numbness take over. Tonight, the numbness isn't coming. Though drugged with exhaustion, the news about his buddies keeps him restive. He decides to dig through his kit. Maybe he'll do some letter writing, although this isn't a good time. He might inadvertently open up to the folks back home. Any hint about the insanity of this place would serve no purpose. Inside his sack, he sees the German - English dictionary he bought before leaving England. He thumbs through the pages. *Sanitäter*, medic.

7. The Aid Station

"MEDIC! MEDIC! For God's sake. For fucking God's sake! Somebody help me! Please!"

The screams of the wounded rise above the battlefield like a refrain from the underworld. Following a failed but bold attempt by a German force to overrun an American position, the odor of phosphorus and charred equipment mingle with the wails of the suffering.

"Please God! Please! Help me, somebody!" shrieks Private Marty Crosby as he grips what's left of one arm with his remaining hand.

In his hysteria, Crosby doesn't realize that lying next to him, face down, is a medic. A German shell had killed a sergeant, blown off Crosby's arm, and driven a piece of metal through the back of the medic's head.

The medic looks gone, but is still breathing. A lieutenant makes an attempt to assist the men, but all he can do is look on in horror, helpless. At that moment, the medic begins to stir. Rather than try to attend to his own head, he focuses on the private. The instinct to save a life helps fight off the shock and pain. He can barely move but begins giving instructions to the officer.

"Get a tourniquet! Use whatever you got!"

Lieutenant Chester Clayman whips the soldier's belt off and begins wrapping it around the stump of the man's mutilated arm. As he tightens the strap, the medic is able to grab a morphine syrette from his kit and hands it to the officer.

"Here, give him a shot. Try the leg." He instructs. Clayman obeys.

"There's sulfa powder in the kit. Find it and sprinkle it on the stump."

Then the medic describes to the lieutenant how to bandage the raw remnant of the arm.

Clayman does as directed. He looks at the infantryman and notices his breathing is now beginning to stabilize. Relieved, he sinks down to catch his breath. The past five hours have been fiendish. Grenades and mortar shells came from nowhere. They poured down from all directions and from both sides. Foxholes changed hands amid close combat. Americans and Germans went at each other with wanton fury. The first to throw a grenade or thrust his bayonet was the one who survived – at least, for the moment.

Clayman had not realized that while he was trying to save his private from bleeding to death, the fighting subsided. He looks around to survey his situation. Above the groans, he sees his men have held. The German attempt to climb the slope to the stronghold has collapsed. Some of his men begin helping with the wounded. Others search through the pockets of enemy dead. Sometimes maps or documents can be useful to G-2 (intelligence). Mostly they find personal letters and photos of loved ones.

Chet Clayman relaxes for a moment, takes off his helmet, and rubs his head. He tries to adjust to the calm. He scans the area wondering where he should start to assess losses when he notices the medic lying lifeless beside him. Clayman leaps to his feet and yells for a Jeep.

"Over here. Help me get these guys on the hood." The two men are placed on the front of the jeep like trophies from a deer hunt.

"When you get to the aid station," he roars, "tell them to send some litter Jeeps."

The aid station is only five hundred yards away. But getting there is a gauntlet of ruts and shell fire. The two men pitch back and forth. They cling to the Jeep as they cling for life.

Aid stations are not behind the lines, they are in the thick of combat. Often aidmen work in bombed out buildings and abandoned bunkers surrounded by exploding mortar shells and hand to hand fighting. Surgeons sometimes operate by flashlight under blankets so as not to give away positions. Unarmed litter bearers risk their lives recovering wounded amid the crossfire.

Rather than wait for supplies, medical units frequently resupply from overrun German positions. The harsh weather and grueling terrain disrupt the supply chain. Troops seize enemy medicines, hospital equipment, and surgical supplies. Once labels are translated, they become stock.

A collection of slouching tents and morose dugouts is behind the hill where Crosby was wounded. GIs lay on the open ground waiting for treatment. They endure their wounds with mostly hushed groans or in stoic silence. Inside the tents the scene is synchronously frantic and efficient. The medical teams have already experienced the worst of the war.

In an operation tent, Greg Towne is working on a soldier with a grotesquely swollen thigh. The GI's fever is hot and his pulse is racing. Penicillin and a bag of blood help to control his pulse rate and blood pressure, but his chances are fading.

"Al!" Towne cries out to his second, "Give me a hand! I don't want to lose this guy!"

Al Jergowsky hands his triage duties off to the nearest man. He runs inside the op tent to assist Towne. It's a dingy dugout of mud and grass floors covered by a frayed canvass tarp, stained with blood. Bellies belch steam as they're sliced. The race to clear the area of filth while casualties mount proceeds in ebbs and flows. A former medical corps officer had described it as a "brown place." "A dirty brown," he said. "A dirty brown, from the doctors, the soldiers, and the wounded. Standards supporting the plasma and blood throw dark brown shadows. Shadows deepen into blocks of darkness,"

Jergowsky looks down at the swollen leg and knows the bulge must be cut open. He hands the surgeon a knife. Towne cuts into the bloated mass and releases a putrid odor of decaying tissue. He cuts away at the grey-pinkish muscle as more gas gangrene fills the tent. The debridement (the surgical art of cutting out dead tissue without mutilating the healthy) extends from the soldier's knee to his hip. But, at least, he will survive. As of a half hour ago, that prospect appeared dim.

His next trip will be to a collection station where his wounds are assessed and cleared for further treatment. If severe enough, his wound may secure him a ticket for evacuation.

Meanwhile, the wounded continue to collect outside the bunker awaiting treatment. "There's only one way to learn surgery…that's to get bloody wet," says another army medical officer. At this aid station, the blood is knee deep. Casualties are sitting, sprawled across litter Jeeps, lying in mud – as the dead pile up.

Eddie Todd who had helped bring Crosby down from the hill, stands by himself, dazed, numbed by the sight of a row of dead GIs. Their bodies are covered and tagged. The stench of death drifts over. Their uniforms and insignias are the same as his. He most likely would recognize the names and some of the faces. Many came from the same part of the country. As he looks down, he asks himself:

"How different are these guys from me? Why are they lying there and am I still standing? Will I be lying there tomorrow? The next day? Next week? Tonight?"

"Todd! Wake up! Get in the goddamn jeep. We're going back to bring in more casualties," screams his sergeant.

Eddie jumps in the litter jeep. "Sarge, I thought I smelled alcohol by the bodies outside that tent. It smelled like whiskey."

"Yeah, I know. That's the burial registration guys. They let them drink so they can stand the smell. They're drunk most of the time, but who here gives a shit?"

Before Todd can process the madness of it all, he notices a metal wire cutter blade welded to the hood of the jeep.

"Hey Sarge, what's with the hood ornament?"

"I'll tell you later."

The sergeant shifts gears into forward, swings the jeep around, and aims it back up towards the hill.

*****

Dear Ann:

I finally got to bed today after a quick meal – going back to work now. It's 10:30 at night. I find it hard sleeping during the day. Unfortunately, night is when the work is done and the men have been shipped off to the clearing stations for more treatment. I've been doing a lot of debridement. Simple but tedious. The war keeps pushing on and every day I tell myself it means we're getting closer to ending this thing. I know we will win in the end, but at a toll. I am well. But if I keep going at this pace, I'll be an old man soon. At least we are moving in the right direction – Berlin.

It's 2230 hours and Greg Towne has worked through the previous night. He tried to get a few hours of sleep during the day – without much success. The casualties keep rolling in. It's time to go back to work. Time to return to the op tents.

"Captain – you wanted to see me?" says Al Jergowsky, entering Towne's tent.

Towne puts his writing aside and looks up at his lieutenant.

"Right, Al. Some admin stuff. Come on in. FYI, we are now part of the 8th Division under British command. Monty needs reinforcement and the army is offering him us. It's just the 311th for now. The 309 and 310 are still part of the 78th. But that will probably change. It's likely they will turn the whole 1st over to him, eventually."

Al shrugs and adds: "As long as we get paid the same, I don't see it mattering to anyone."

Greg Towne smirks, and adds, "Since Jerry's offensive has halted at Dinant, the whole front is scrambling to counterattack. We've held and are the northern shoulder of the salient. There are just two divisions still inside Germany. We're one of them. It looks like we'll be on the Siegfried Line…part of the spearhead to break out to take the bridges and dams."

Al nods and asks, "Anything else Captain?"

"Yeah. It's why I really need to talk to you. There's gonna be a ceasefire in a day or two. The Bosch are proposing a truce to see to the wounded. We should get the details soon – maybe in a couple of hours."

"The 28th was part of one in November."

"Yeah, the Germans proposed that one too." Towne nods. "It's along the Kall forge trail again. Just like the one back then, except this time it's unofficial. Moving in and out of there could be one big FUBAR."

"Unofficial? Damn! Plus, the terrain's impossible." Jergowsky breathes out sharply.

"Impossible! It's a God-damn dog breakfast."

"I'll let the guys know," says Jergowsky.

"Try to sound optimistic," Towne tells him, half-sarcastically. He leans back against a tent pole and stretches out his long legs.

Towne comes from a clan of Philadelphia Brahmins. He's a third-generation Dartmouth man and a second-generation physician. Despite his pedigree and education, he's never lost his common touch. Gregory Towne is as comfortable in a south Philly working man's bar as he is in the plush, polished Union League lounge. His wiry frame and aristocratic features set him apart, but his patrician looks mask an impatience with pretense and pomp. He is known by patients for his upbeat bedside manner. However, among the elite he has a reputation for being direct, brusque, and often snarky.

He met his wife during his residency where she was a nurse. Before the war, their futures appeared cemented in a life of comfort and privilege. Then came Pearl Harbor. He could have accepted the occupational deferment arranged by his medical center. Instead, he chose to serve at the front at a time when the army desperately needed doctors, and recruited medical students. He avoided his local draft board and enlisted through another in order to stanch the protests of hospital administrators. By the end of the war, he will have conducted hundreds of surgeries and treated countless other casualties – including "psychological ineffectives."

"Al, I'm sorry for unloading on you the other day. I've just seen too many of our boys torn to pieces. I reached a breaking point and …."

He breathes a faint groan and stares vacantly at the air in front of him. "I had a kid here the other day. He was about 21 years old and hadn't yet met his new baby. He asked me to stay by him during his final hours. He was slipping in and out of consciousness. Sometimes he thought he was at home on his farm. Other times he was aware and understood he would never see his little girl. That's when he would beg us not to let him die. But within hours – he was gone. What are you supposed to do? Do you say, "So what! Just another casualty, another battle statistic. Try not feel anything, just to keep going? Is that the person you have to become?" He shakes his head. "Not me…not me."

Towne pauses. "Sometimes I feel as old as Methuselah, and think I can't see another kid die."

Al looks down at the floor recalling the young German whose life he tried to save. After a moment, Al says to him: "Greg, you're a good doctor. I've learned a lot working with you – not just about this." He gestures upward to the horrid and grotesque world of the aid station.

"I mean that…for what it's worth." He hesitates and then continues: "We will all be different once this is over. I also believe that, God willing, we will be stronger for it. And, I can't imagine serving with anyone else."

Al sighs and laments: "I just would never want to do it again."

Towne's shoulders sag. He tightens his lips and nods humbly for a few moments: "Well." He straightens back up and grabs a pack of cigarettes from off his desk. "I gotta go to work."

The captain pushes himself out of wooden chair: "I'll see you later?"

"You bet," Jergowsky answers.

Before Al reaches the flap leading to the outside of the tent, Dr. Towne calls out: "Hey, Al."

Jergowsky stops and turns.

"Thanks Al, for everything."

"Always," says his lieutenant.

Outside the captain's tent, Jergowsky walks to where his sergeant and several medics are hanging.

"Any scuttlebutt Lieutenant?" asks one of the aidmen.

"Yeah" he tells them. "As of now we are under Montgomery's command."

"Well, fuck me sideways and call me Skippy," one of the medics pipes up. He tries to laugh but the silence suggests no one is in the mood for humor.

"I'll try to remember that, Lowery," says Jergowsky.

He reaches for a pack of cigarettes from his jacket pocket, pulls out a stick, and lights up.

"There's something else." He breathes out a puff. "There's going to be a ceasefire either tomorrow or the next day. We'll be taking in casualties and clearing the dead from the Kall trail. As you know, getting in and out of there will be a real snake wedding."

Frank Murphy adds, "Yeah. In addition to a lot of abandoned equipment and downed trees, there's the slope."

There's nothing but silence until someone asks: "Has anyone told the artillery?"

"Just pray they have. As far as I understand, this truce isn't officially recognized."

An uncomfortable stir and the hum of grumbling whirrs within the tight crowd. "FUBAR," the men murmur.

"In the meantime, just make sure everyone has their Geneva Convention Cards. Jerry will be checking for them." Then Al turns and looks at Don Lowery: "That goes for you, too…Skippy."

8. The Ceasefire

"This is worse than I imagined."

Captain Klaus Haas, a German medical officer, surveys the landscape along the Kall River gorge. In swirling snow, friend and foe, dead and wounded, lie beside each other. Men are lumped together between shot out vehicles. The split and twisted bodies expose rotting internal organs. Survivors huddle in muddy foxholes, soaked and starving – in some cases, sobbing.

Earthworms wriggle in the water and ditches. The sight of them is unnerving, freakish – a constant reminder of death. Soldiers imagine what will become of their own remains. They kill the squalid creatures with rifle butts. The air has become sick with the stench of rotting flesh.

In this cesspit of carrion and degradation, the wounded regard uniforms with indifference. Uniforms are meaningless, if even identifiable under the blood and mud.

"Do we have enough translators?" asks Haas.

"Two of the men speak English, and the pastors makes four, *Hauptmann*," reports his *Oberleutnant*.

"Nah gut. The Americans will have more. Thanks to their Yids."

He scans the trail where he expects the Americans to show. "I read that Americans like to call themselves a nation of immigrants." He observes the American dead. "A nation of immigrants, indeed." His face gets grim. "In the last century, they were a nation of slaves." And he adds: "They are just as racist and anti-Semitic as anyone." Have a sentry notify me when they finally arrive."

Klaus Haas grew up in Munich during the rise of the National Socialist German Workers' Party. His father was a lawyer and his mother a school administrator. Although the nationalism appealed to Haas, his medical ambitions and Catholic upbringing restrained him. "I have plenty of masters already," he complained.

Haas has had enough propaganda and war by 1944. His loyalty is to the German people, particularly the victimized and vulnerable. After two years at the Eastern front, campaigns in Italy, and along the *Westwall*, he believes in nothing. His religion is cynicism. He hates the regime, but does not trust the Allies. And, his country is still at war, no matter how hopeless, no matter how wrong.

"Do we know when our artillery barrages will begin again?" asks the oberleutnant.

"No one has told us yet." The doctor looks at his junior officer with as much sympathy as he can muster. "Brandt, if there is one thing I've learned in my brief military career, it's that war is much more waiting than fighting."

He looks back at the trail, "Considerably more. And sometimes, the wait is far worse than the fight."

Just then a column of U.S. troops approaches, unarmed and wearing Red Cross armbands. Only the officers are bearing side arms.

A convoy of ambulances halts. An officer leaps out of the lead vehicle. A junior officer accompanies him.

"I'm Captain Douglas Talbot. Here are my credentials. I believe you will see everything is in order." He speaks in perfect German as he hands his counterpart his ID papers and Geneva Convention card.

The *Wehrmacht* officer glances back at the *Oberleutnant*, affirms the documentations, and returns them with his own. The American nods to acknowledge.

"Your German is very good, Captain. Where did you learn it? Are either of your parents German?"

"University" replies Talbot. "We have them in the States, despite rumors to the contrary." Doug Talbot knows he's taking a swipe at the Nazi theory of *Herrenrasse*, but he enjoys treating arrogance with sarcasm at every opportunity, even when unprompted. "Furthermore, it's a simple language."

The German breathes in deeply and stares at the American briefly. By now, the veteran soldier has learnt when and where to pick his battles; besides, there is work to be done. He allows Talbot to have the last word.

He grudgingly admits to himself the forceful impression left by Talbot. This American is arrogant, willful and pigheaded. But he is also educated, and likely competent. A "citizen soldier", in American terminology, who would have probably made a fine German officer. But the generally held belief, which has been drummed into the popular psyche, is that European castoffs built America. Its early rise was buttressed by institutional slavery. No professional warrior class, a country of gangsters, mixed races, self-indulgence, and a cripple as its President – this is no match for the *Reich*. On the other hand, many Americans are of German blood. And, they are led by a man named Eisenhower.

Before the two captains finish their salutes, the medics from both sides start working on the wounded. Soon makeshift shelters are being built to cover the triage. Soldiers use Red Cross flags and blankets to protect men on the ground from the snow and drizzle. A cave-like 18-by-12-foot dugout sits precariously in the steep hillside that borders the trail. The hut is filled with casualties and medics, who remained behind after the fighting. They would either be relieved or continue to care for the wounded into the POW camps.

Steadily, the hiss of gasoline lanterns rises, bringing light into the interiors. Americans and Germans huddle together to share the warmth of each other's bodies. At last, they are getting attention – from both medical teams.

Many are reduced to lost boys, disoriented and afraid. Others abandon themselves to their destinies. "The sooner you realized you were here to be killed, the better," goes one adage about Hürtgen Forest.

Away from the joint aid station, Frank Murphy is cutting away a trouser leg to examine a sergeant who had his leg torn apart by mortar shell. As Murphy cleanses the opening, the soldier tosses his head back and forth muttering: "They're killing my boys, they're killing my boys."

Lying next to Murphy, a *Wehrmacht* soldier is asking the medic, "Is my arm gone? Tell me the truth." Another begs: "Comrades, please shoot me!" Men want to know if they will survive, they pray, and slip in and out of consciousness.

A medic is applying a compress and patches from his own coat to a sucking chest wound. All around are the murmur of groans and pleas. The appeals to God throb beneath the distant rumble of cannon fire, the growl of orders, and cries for morphine, plasma, drugs, dressings, sulfa, splints, and litter bearers.

In the dim of the forest, medics and surgeons run their hands over ruptured areas to analyze the trauma. "It's like putting your hands in buckets of wet liver," said a veteran. Litter carriers slog through mud to load men onto ambulances. The faces of the wounded are often either bloody or bloodless, while the faces of the dead take on a deep claret hue as their capillaries freeze.

Several hours in, Haas is working under a lean-to shanty made from a discarded parachute. On a blood-soaked ground cover, a German soldier lies with his wound rupturing. A gash from a grenade fragment is now splitting apart, exposing his intestines.

"*Sanitäter!*" Haas screams as he holds the corporal's lacerations closed with both hands. "I need help. Now!"

Although the man is turning white, he still has a chance. Before Haas can take his eyes off the young soldier, another pair of hands holds the torn flesh closed.

"I got him," says Al Jergowsky in broken German.

Haas nods thankfully.

The two men work together in silence, using body language and gestures to communicate. Their shared training and battlefield experience allow them to operate concordantly.

Jergowsky and Haas swab, clean, and disinfect the wound. Behind the shroud of morphine looms agony. Thankfully, the boy has passed out. The soldier's breathing is hurried, but steady. Gradually and expertly the lacerations are being closed and dressed. A life is saved.

Haas checks his vital signs. Jergowsky leaves the tent and waves over two Yank litter bearers. "Take this guy to the German side."

The men gently roll the soldier on to the stretcher and carry him in the direction of a Jerry ambulance. Jergowsky turns back to Haas. He nods and the two men part to attend to others.

It's becoming darker. The rescue operation has been going on without interruption for over five hours. The Kall Trail, already dimmed by the thick forest, is fading to black. The medical teams have loaded the wounded onto every available vehicle. On both sides, men are exhausted. Everyone is cold and wet. All the while, the sounds of artillery and mortar fire have been closing in. The shelling is becoming more intense. Artillery shells are landing within yards of the makeshift op. tents and remaining vehicles. One shell drops next to an American jeep and riddles the vehicle with fragments.

"Cease operations!"

Talbot screams to his men, "Button it up! We're getting out of here!" He runs in, out, and between huddles of medics hurrying applications of the last dressings, moving bodies onto litters, and piling non-walking wounded into vehicles.

Haas is ordering his men back to their lines. Suddenly, another blast forces him to dive into a bomb crater. When the bombardment momentarily stops, Haas finds himself lying next to a dead American soldier. He gazes at the soldier, who is no more than a teenager. His open mouth seems to demand to know the justification for the horror, the barbarism. At the same time, he seems to also be looking to God for mercy.

Haas prays: "Dear God, is there a mother somewhere in America to mourn this boy? Or, is it better there be no mother left alive to grieve? Hasn't there already been enough sorrow?"

Haas runs to join his men. As he makes toward the staff car, he sees Jergowsky directing his men toward the opposite direction.

"*Leutnant*!"

Jergowsky turns to the sound of Haas's voice.

Haas walks at him.

"Lieutenant, in memory of this day." Klaus Haas removes his medical field kit from his pack and hands it to Al Jergowsky. Al takes it in to his hand and then salutes.

"*Danke, Kapitän.*"

"*Danke, Leutnant.*"

They part. Haas rides away in his staff car. The vehicle tosses and thrashes over the rutted ground. He grips the car as it jostles away from the approaching bombardment. He is exhausted to the point of confusion. Yesterday it was all-out war. Today was an act of humanity. So many times during this war he has felt torn between yesterday and today. Suspended somewhere between his duty as a *Wehrmacht* officer and his oath as a doctor. Where does one end and the other begin? The battleground in this conflict is his own human heart. For now, the outcome in that struggle is deferred. The only apt thought that keeps pulsing in his head are words from his catechism: "In the fullness of time, all shall be revealed."

Al jumps in the back of the jeep where Frank Murphy is waiting for him.

"What that, Lieutenant?"

"I guess you could call it a party favor."

Al looks over the dark horizon where Haas's car has now disappeared. He scans the dense gloom and whispers to himself: "*L'chaim, Kapitän*!…To life!

*****

Several days later, in an abandoned house. men are playing cards, reading their mail, talking and writing letters. It's the first hard protection from the elements many of these Doughs have had in weeks. A soldier-poet writes: "For a moment, the war surrenders…. And the world is made human, again."

Canteens filled with kerosene stuffed with socks for wicks light the rooms. A soldier writes to his wife: "The mere sound of a flush toilet is like music. Such small pleasures are to cherish."

Al Jergowsky is reading a letter a from home and smiling. One of the men notices and prods him to open up. "Hey Lieutenant, good news? You look like you won the lottery."

Another grumbles aloud: "We all did. How do you think we got here?"

Over the sarcastic snicks, Al tells them, "No, nothing that good. It's just a letter from my sister"

"She's not pregnant, is she Lieutenant?"

"No, Delaney, she's saving herself for you," Al says, while still staring down at the letter.

"She works for Benny Goodman's music company. We all went to school with Frank Sinatra in Hoboken. She just wrote to say he dropped by and asked about me. That's all."

"That's all!"

"Lieutenant! You've been holding out on us. You and Frank S."

"Relax, It's no big deal.   Hoboken is one square mile. Everybody knows everybody"

"Shit," says Art Russo. "The closest I ever came to a celebrity was at a Jeep Show. I think the guy's name was Red Bottoms."

"Buttons, you idiot.   His name was Red Buttons." Delaney growls.

"Hey, Lieutenant, what did you do before the war?"

"I worked for Warner Brothers." Al tells Delaney, while still looking down at the letter.

"Holy shit! It gets better!" cries Russo.

"Don't get excited fellas. I was in the accounting office. I didn't touch any stars. I counted beans."

"Still," says Delaney. "Just being close to a Rockette would make me faint right now. You gonna back to your old job after the war, Lieutenant?"

"I don't know Joe. I'll take it one step at a time. What about you? Whatta you gonna do?"

"I figure I'd go back to Pittsburgh. Open a hardware store. My high school team was the Dragons. 'Dragon Hardware' ought a bring in the crowds. That's the plan."

"Sounds like a plan."

"Cars!" says Don Lowery.

"Cars?"

"Oh yeah, cars, automobiles, trucks…There's gonna be a big demand when this war is over. Once GM, Chrysler, and Ford are done building tanks, they gotta go back to building cars, and lots of them. Have you seen what the Germans have? The Good Ole' USA will be there. There's going to be a lot of money to be made."

"Jesus Christ, Lowery! I underestimated you. That almost sounds brilliant. You're nowhere as dumb as you look," says Al

"I know!" beams Lowery.

"You might have given me my next post-war fantasy."

Al notices Herb Boyd. Herb is a shy kid. He rarely speaks and often has to be prodded. He follows orders, puts himself in his job, and never complains.

"What about you Herb? Got any plans for after the war?" asks Jergowsky

Boyd breathes in a full breath and humbly says: "Yeah, once I get back to my town in West Virginia, I'm never leaving." He shakes his head and adds, "I'm gonna ask a girl name Rose if she still wants to get married. And if she does, that's where I'm stayin'. I've seen enough of this world to last me a lifetime. To know knowledge is to know sorrow, says the Bible. I've learned my lesson fellas."

Several men nod.

"Not me." Walter Sozek is from Zion, Illinois. Sozek was drafted straight out of high school. He was witness to interrogations of wounded German prisoners, and even took part once he became familiar with the language. The horror and the human side of the war fascinate him, more than he wants to admit. For him, there has to be something more than the feeling of doing one's duty. He had helped send men back into action, physically able but psychologically spent. They may have survived and slogged on, but they performed their duties without being able to define them.

"I want to learn more," Walt explains. "I got a lot of questions coming out of this war. If they give me a chance, I'll go back to school. You never know about the future, boys. I wasn't prepared for this, and I just want to be prepared for what's coming next."

Al nods. "What would you study if you went back?"

"Well, I've been thinking about medical school. Why not? I can do debridement in my sleep, and I've seen enough trauma to write a book."

"Maybe you should take up psychiatry. In the next war, you can analyze the enemy to death," says Lowery.

"Yeah. Living with you has been a regular internship…Skippy," sniffs Sozek.

Al sees that Frank Murphy has been quiet. He's been sitting on the floor, expressionless, with his back against the wall. It's usually not like him to be indifferent. Tonight, he looks anesthetized as he stares into nowhere.

"What about you Murph? What are your plans after the war?" asks Al.

Frank lifts his head up. His eyes have the appearance of raw bankruptcy.

"Me? What am I gonna do after the war?" He groans. "The first thing I'm gonna do when I get back to Texas is…cry a bucket of tears."

9. Winter, 1945

David Jergowsky is sitting in the same chair where he sits every night. Usually, he is checking his mail or reading the paper. Tonight, he's doing neither. He is still, barely concentrating. Recollection of untroubled times play in his mind. They summon memories of trips to ballgames, museums, birthday parties, and the joy of watching your child laugh and play. The February air outside the snug home in his Queens neighborhood is freezing, and he worries if his son Al has shelter. Is he healthy? Is he scared? Is he…David doesn't dare finish the next thought.

Abruptly, his trance is disrupted by a gentle tapping on the doorway of his study.

"Come on in, Doc."

Doctor Abe Hankins steps in and takes a seat on the sofa opposite David.

"Chaya will be fine. Just a cold. Probably aggravated by stress. She'll live. A more important question is…How are you doing?"

"Me?"

"You. You look tired, worn. I think we should make an appointment for you. This has been harder on you than your wife. I know you well, Dave. You tend to keep things inside. It's eating at you."

"It's eating all of us. Everyone has aged. We've lost contact with the family back in the old country. But we also know why."

Doctor Hankins eases his bulky frame against the back of the sofa. He takes off his glasses and speaks softly as he cleans the lenses. "I know. There's a lot of good boys over there. They're winning, but they're paying, too." He heaves a sigh. For a moment he, too, reflects on better times.

David looks up with a taut expression that's holding back tears. "You know, my boy is the toughest, sweetest kid there's ever been. I worried how he and Florence would fit in this new and strange place. But, before I realized it, I was the father of the all-American kid. He made friends easily. He excelled at school. He even skipped a grade."

Dr. Hankins smiles warmly. He knows that letting his patient speak openly is good therapy. He's never known his friend to brag or breathe a word about a loss. Now, he's letting go. To have someone to listen is a blessing.

"It seemed like this America was made for him. I brought them here as little foreigners, and this country claimed them as her own."

David's lips faintly tremble and his eyes start to water. He fights off the emotions and thinks back.

"Al got a full scholarship to Stevens Tech, Abe. The principal of his high school begged him to take it. Columbia wanted him, too. But he went to CCNY."

"The 'Poor man's Harvard'."

David nods. "He went to CCNY so he could work full-time. Before we knew it, he had 12 auditors reporting to him, even though he was just a kid out of high school. With it all, he still found time for the boxing team at college." David smiles. "Even had a shot at the Golden Gloves. He loved boxing, but his mother and I worried about him. Imagine, worrying about something as slight as that." He shakes his head.

"I know, Dave. I remember when we went to one of Al's bouts. He sure had quick hands."

"I know, but I was almost glad when he went up against someone with a quicker pair. It finally ended his secret dream of being the next Jewish lightweight champion."

"Another Benny Leonard, right?"

Both chuckle.

David can't remember talking this much. He realizes that he's letting go of the things he's been wanting to say out loud for years. But the future is unknown, and why deny himself? The least he can do is admit his pride in Al. David is the kind of parent who has always been too humble to boast. He scorned swagger. When he saw those traits in others, he would indulge them. He smiled fondly to himself and understood how pleased these parents must be to have an audience, even though it may go against his own nature. For him, now, the chance to speak adoringly about his son feels like a confession as much as a sort of self-praise. And so, he goes on.

"You know, he didn't wait to finish his last year in college. He didn't even wait for Pearl Harbor. He enlisted in August."

Doc Hankins chimes in. "I remember how proud we were when he came home after graduating from Officer Candidate School."

David nods. "Finished the top of his class at OCS."

Hankins smiles and says, "If anyone can survive this war, it will be Al."

"Right. I'd even say he might have a better chance than we do."

The friends smile. Dr. Hankins lifts himself from the sofa and puts his hand on David's shoulder. "Keep well David. He's coming home. Just make sure you make that appointment with Ruthie. Keep in mind, this war is almost over. You just have to hold on."

"I know. But sometimes I think the waiting is worse than the fighting," sighs David

"I know, I know."

Hankins picks up his bag. "Sit. I can show myself out. Call me if you need anything. I'm always here.

"Thanks Abe. Keep well yourself."

David's thoughts and emotions can't stop swirling. He blows out a puff of air, then rises to turn on the radio. Maybe there is good news from the front.

*****

Eddie Todd is sitting in the snow along a trail near the German town of Schmidt. In the early morning hours, at approximately 0300, an artillery barrage took out half of his platoon. The survivors learned that they were not German shells, but an American battery test firing.

There is no time to mourn the tragedy. You grumble FUBAR and keep moving.

Along the way, they pass a graveyard of broken weapons, discarded equipment, and abandoned tanks that hang precariously over cliffs above the Kall forge. Strewn among the wreckage are the bodies of GIs and Germans, frozen since November. They lie there as a result of an attempt by the Americans to take the high-ground overlooking the river. Germans retain control of the town that guards access to the Schwammenauel Dam. In place, still, are the landmines.

"Saddle up!" Todd falls in Indian-style formation with the rest of the battalion. The path forward is steep. Men ascend by holding on to tree limbs and pulling themselves up a few feet at a time. They drag combat packs, mortars, and machine guns as they climb. Every several minutes they stop to rest.

Suddenly, up ahead, Eddie hears small-arms fire. He can hear the exchange between M1s and *Wehrmacht* 98Ks. You learn to distinguish their sounds and get a sense for which side has the greater fire power and who might be the ones taken by surprise. He hears only the M1s, and assumes it's the Americans who have the jump. Once the fire ceases, he hears men yelling.

Looking up the hill, he sees a German soldier being led down the line. His wounds are grave. The slope is steep. He's blind. Each man takes a turn guiding him to the next man below. Through the heavily wooded descent, the doughs pass him on from one to another. As the German gets nearer to Eddie, he sees how serious his wounds are. "Poor bastard," he murmurs to himself. "Will he even make it to a medic?"

Todd grasps his trembling hand, and with the other hand takes his arm. He's muttering incoherently. His face is torn apart and his field-gray uniform is shredded. He passes the moaning soldier to the next man below. He may be the enemy, but he's still a human being – what's left of one.

As the German moves further down the line, the march toward Schmidt resumes. The men strain under the weight of their gear. They've come through the early hours, the darkness, cold, heart-breaking terrain, minefields veiled by snow, and their own artillery to engage the enemy. They now face the devilish pillboxes. There is no talking, only the sound of men struggling over slick and tangled ground laden with their packs.

Unexpectedly, a shot rings out behind Todd.

There's silence as the men look at one another with the same questioning gaze. Someone breaks the silence with a single word. "Malmedy"

The nearest man to Eddie looks at him and whispers, "You don't think somebody..."

Another overhears. "Why not? He's a Kraut, ain't he?"

Ahead, still lies the mission. The goal which seemed so far away in December is within the clutch of the 1st Army. Weariness is thrust aside. This is no time for respite. The enemy is in retreat, and the attack to capture Schmidt and clear the way into Germany is underway.

Victory is coming closer, but at what price no one knows.

Todd hikes up his gear and restarts his crawl to the summit. He's thankful he was not a witness to the killing. He consoles himself by thinking that perhaps it was an act of mercy, not a simple murder. Some men will return home from this day. They will recall the barrage from their own artillery, the murderous climb, and the attack. And some will also remember the unknown soldier's red hair, his youthful and disfigured face, his ragged battle fatigues, the way he held out his hand seeking help, comfort, grasping the nearest hand to lead him to safety. And, they will remember how his end came.

These images will seep into dreams at night, haunt quiet moments as they flicker and fade, ambush idle thoughts without forewarning. For the men who felt sympathy for the *Wehrmacht* soldier, he will become part of their lives. He may be gone, but he will never leave. As fathers and grandfathers, every time they see a young man with red hair they might go back to the day outside of Schmidt.

In another area of the sector, Al Jergowsky and Frank Murphy are patrolling in their litter Jeep looking for wounded. It's an anguished job in a grim place. Months ago, an infantryman from the 1st Army lost part of his leg when he stepped on a German *Schümine*. The explosion cauterized the arteries, so he lay conscious for three days along the side of a trail. The men in his unit could not reach him because of withering enemy fire. But the *Wehrmacht* did. Two Germans crawled their way over treacherous ground. When they made it to where he was lying, they removed his field jacket and helmet and left a booby trap under his back. He lay helpless and alert long enough to ward off the medics.

The Americans develop similar techniques as they, too, go about the business of war. A diary of a lieutenant in the Ardennes read: "Some of our best men are the most murderous." Extending across the heroism, the battles for the Ardennes and Hürtgen are driven by desperation and revenge.

Al and Frank are silent as they make it across the battle zone, scanning the area for wounded and any hints of an enemy gun position. Frank drives his Jeep across the rutted ground, avoiding the humps that might conceal a landmine. The path of the Jeep is erratic. Murphy loses control when the vehicle slips sideways over frozen and muddy patches. Then the last thing that both men remember is the deafening sound of an explosion, as they are being lifted into the air and thrown from the Jeep. The Jeep spins like a whirligig in midair. It crashes to the earth in flames. Al and Frank's bodies land on the ground. They lie there bloody and motionless.

Several days later, Greg Towne asks, "Any news about Lt. Jergowsky and Murph?"

"Nothing, Captain," Walt Sozek tells him.

Towne looks off in the distance as Sozek stares at the ground.

"You gonna report them as MIA, Sir?"

"Yeah. We have no choice."

Maybe the Tommies picked them up. You don't know."

"Where there's life, there's hope, right? Meanwhile, it's another two letters from the War Department."

Later that night, Dr. Greg Towne writes a letter to his wife. Half way through, his writing turns to rants: "I'm weary of the clamor of war. I'm tired of the stress, the hunger, the bloodthirst…"

He stops, drops his pen, breathes in, and tears up the letter.

10. "At least their mothers can't see them when they die"

Hitler's grand gamble in the Ardennes has failed. Since December 27th, 1944, the Germans have been in retreat. Towns come and go while men die in the thousands. Bodies are everywhere...bloated and floating in rivers, rotting in bunkers and foxholes, seared inside tanks, sprawled across streets, hanging from trees. One rifleman pauses to catch his breath during the fight for a town, lights a cigarette, and discovers what he thought was rubble is a pile of twisted frozen *Landsers*.

Soldiering involves living through one of the harshest winters in history. Surviving on congealed hash rather than solid food. Sleeping in concrete bunkers, icy foxholes, across the front seat of damp trucks. Meanwhile, the dread uncertainty of life exceeds the fear of death. Raindrops sound like sinister step falls. The rustling of trees, the movement of an invader. Behind these figments, a savage death looms.

Despite victory being within their grasp, weary combat troops are impassive, languid, withdrawn. An infantryman writes to his wife: "My mind is absolutely stripped of any reason for war." A survivor of an assault on a section of the Siegfried Line asks: "What are they saving me for?" Before he can descend into a downward spiral of survivor guilt, another man answers: "The Pacific."

Chet Clayman is leading a patrol through Schmidt. He's already lost several of his men to snipers. A particularly pesky one has been registering kills for several days. His MO is to wait, kill, and move. Officers, communications men, and other high-value targets are prime prey.

Snipers live by a different code than other troops. In the American army, they are volunteers. The *Wehrmacht* conscripts them. More than simply marksmen, they are hunters. Their craft involves stalking, preparing escape holes, and leaving behind booby traps for their trackers. The loss of a buddy to a sniper's bullet is taken personally. General Omar Bradley declares: "I will not take action against any soldier that had treated a sniper roughly." His words, though made in private, have consequences. A sniper who was taken prisoner in a town of the Ardennes was tied to a tree. Imagine his final thoughts when a Sherman tank moved in and lowered its gun at him.

Clayman and his sergeant are moving in and out of demolished structures looking for traces of the sniper who killed their radio man and several non-coms. The shapeless forms and smoking rockery that was once a town offers excellent cover. The two men from the 311th press themselves against outer walls and crawl between shelled homes. Their pursuit brings them to one of the last standing buildings in Schmidt – a church.

They enter from opposite sides of the altar. Clayman surveys the rows of pews as Sgt. Pete Sosnowski investigates the sacristy. Slowly they begin to move down the length of the nave checking the ranks of benches. When they reach the back, Clayman yells out to Sosnowski, "Nothing here, let's move out."

Sosnowski nods calmly. He raises his Browning Automatic Rifle and levels it at the confessional. He empties the magazine. The booth explodes into pieces of shard wood. Out of the "dark box" a German soldier tumbles onto the floor and covers it with blood.

Clayman looks vacantly at the dead body and exits the church without a word. Sosnowski stays behind. He turns back toward the front of the church and looks up at the Christ figure hovering above the tabernacle. He can't help but be heart-struck by the suffering image hanging from the cross. Mechanically, he utters words from Luke: Father, forgive them. He removes his helmet and makes the sign of the cross before he, too, leaves to join his men.

While the town is being secured, Ed Todd is manning a gun position outside Schmidt. He scans dark earthy craters, bullet-riddled trees, and dead Yanks. The scars of three days of fighting. Several yards from him, a Graves Registration detail is gathering men from the assault force. The grave team goes about their work with a hardened detachment, each man managing the unbearable job in his own way. Many have been drinking. They throw the corpses onto a truck like cordwood.

Schmidt had become an abattoir where the men who sacrificed their lives are treated like meat. Bodies pile up on the truck bed behind the driver. The dead GIs are flat on the ground, with one exception. A lone soldier is lying on his side with his arm slightly raised above his head. They place him atop the heap.

Weighed down with cargo, the Jimmy begins to move out over the ruts and gullies. It passes in front of Todd's gun position. As it rocks back and forth, Todd's fallen "friend" appears to wave goodbye. Ed's eyes follow him until the truck is out of sight. The image will remain. Forty-five years later, Todd will tell the story of the waving soldier. By then, the nameless trooper will have been a life-long companion.

The recovery of the wounded and dead continues. A large bomb crater is functioning as an aid station. The harvest of casualties has been from three days of mortar fire, machine gun nests, snipers, mine fields, and hand-to-hand, eye-to-eye combat.

"You got him?" grunts Walt Sozek to Don Lowery as they lift a wounded rifleman strapped to a litter. He is brought out of the crater and loaded on an ambulance headed for the collection station. From there he will go to an evacuation hospital. The war is over for him.

"You're going home buddy," Lowery tells the wounded Joe.

The soldier brims with joy and gives the medic a thumbs-up. Lowery returns the gesture with a nod. One of the guys passes by and gives the man a good luck pat.

"Take care, pal."

"You are going to be alright. You made it!" Don continues to offer encouragement to the GI, who is no more than 19 years old. He had been at the front after only a few months of basic training. During his short time in combat, he saw a lot of his friends die. Some, he never learned their full names.

"Yeah, I made it."

The ambulance doors swing open and the driver helps bring the litter onboard. Sozek slams the door shut and gives it a final spank before it moves away. He and Lowery watch as the war-scarred Chevy lumbers its way towards the rear.

"Ever see someone so happy to lose a leg?" says Sozek to Lowery.

"Maybe? What would you give to go home?"

"Depends on what day. Some days, just about anything."

"There's going to be a lot more like him. Those *Schümines* are everywhere. Plus, metal detectors don't work because the detonator is inside a wooden box. Also, the krauts replace them as soon as…"

"Jesus Christ! Axis Sally! I don't need a pep talk right now. Fucking Little Miss Sunshine!"

"I'm just saying…"

There's a stir in the aid station hole, a flurry of men scrambling to pack up equipment.

"C'mon you guys. We're moving up," yells Joe Delaney.

"Where to?"

"Schmidt. They've cleared the town…what's left of it."

"I'll get some kits," says Walt. "Grab your gear, Skippy."

"I hate that name," grumbles Lowery.

A column of infantrymen, combat engineers and medics moves forward. Before them is a gauntlet of shelling, small and heavy gun fire, and landmines. Engineers have marked off paths with white tape. But the Germans have become expert at allowing invading forces to pass by and then slip in new mines after roadways have been cleared. They often obscure the new diggings by dragging detached axles with wheels over the fresh placements.

The troops tread a scarred earth: deformed by endless shelling. Night vistas that could rival scenes from Dante's Inferno erupt before the eyes. Flares and tracer fire from small arms flood a topography of mud, snow, and death. The arcing fire mingles with artillery flares and the howl of battle. A panorama of horror and eerie beauty engulf the consciousness. How one survives such convulsion is a matter of luck.

The next day, the column marches past an un-marked minefield. In the middle of the patch, a wounded man lies in shock, groaning with his foot blown away. The blast killed his buddy instantly, picked him up, threw him 20 feet through the air. While in mid-air, the shell fragments peppered his body; one piece severed his foot and another hit the bone behind his right ear after piercing his helmet. He's pleading and sobbing. All anyone can do is watch and listen to his pleas. The Captain yells "Keep moving!" Gradually, the crying stops and his sobs give way to prayers.

"I can't bear to hear one more guy in agony. No more!" mutters Lowery.

"What are you talking about?", asks Sozek who is trailing behind.

"No more. I hear them every night."

Before anyone can stop him. Don Lowery begins crossing over the minefield towards the suffering infantryman. The column halts. Every eye is on Lowery.

"Get back here," yells the captain. "That's an order!"

"Don! Stop! We can't lose you!" shouts Sozek and Delaney.

"Sorry guys. It's my job," Lowery hollers back.

"No, it's not," bellows Sozek. "No, it's not!"

Don Lowery picks his way through field, looking for any hint or suggestion of a horrid death. As he stalks his way through the murderous maze, he begins saying his own prayers: "Yea, I walk through the shadow of the valley of death, I will fear no evil: for thou art with me; thy rod and thy staff they comfort me…"

An explosion blows him in the air like a rag doll. His legs separate from his body. What's left of Don Lowery falls to ground. Everyone waits for something to happen next. What happens next is indelible, haunting. After a few minutes, the nightmare continues. Lowery regains consciousness and resumes clawing his way toward the wounded man. He inches forward, and continues to pray to himself: "You prepare a table before me in the presence of my enemies. You anoint my head with oil; my cup runneth…"

Finally, the end comes. Lowery pulls himself over a second mine. What's left of his torso is blasted into carnage. There is nothing but an uneasy silence. Each man retreats to his own world.

After the momentary quiet, the captain sends a runner for a mine disposal team.

"Move out." He yells.

The troops move in formation in silence towards the sounds of the distant fire. The replacements lurch forward still in disbelief. Moments like these turn young men into combat veterans…boys from sheltered homes learn to kill without emotion, without hating. Those who have witnessed such scenes before, fume with rage. Some of them find a calling – killing Krauts.

The next German captured or attempts to surrender will suffer a fate, in part, due to Lowery's sacrifice. Killing will become an obsession for some. Naked revenge a force. A lieutenant recorded in his diary:

> We found fifteen Germens cowering in a crater in the forest. Their

visible wish to surrender – most were in tears with terror and de-
spair – was ignored by our men lining the rim…laughing and howling, hoo-ha-ing and cowboy and good-old-boy yelling our men ex-
ultingly shoot into the crater until every single man down there was
dead…the result was deep satisfaction.

Back home, Don Lowery's family will receive the notice from the
War Department. They remember and cherish a boy who wanted to
please, to see people smile. That was ripped from them. Left behind
are memories, his Silver Star, and the sadness of another unfulfilled
life.

*****

"Leftenant. Leftenant. Can you hear me? Are you awake? How do
you feel?"

Al Jergowsky is coming out of a deep sleep. He hears a female
voice but he can't quite make out what she's saying. He's groggy. His
eyesight is faint. His head is throbbing. He has no idea where he is.

As his senses gradually regain their properties, he registers the
woman's voice as soothing, reassuring. She speaks with a British ac-
cent.

"How do you feel?"

Al opens his eyes.   He can see he's in a medical ward. The nurse
waits for him. Al attempts to raise himself from his bed, but the
nurse gently places her hand on his shoulder.

"Rest, Leftenant. You need your rest.   You've been in and out for
a couple of days."

She sees his confusion and fluster.

"One of our patrols picked you up several days ago. Your Jeep,
evidently, either ran over a land mine or was hit by a mortar shell.
You took some nasty nicks and bruises, but nothing that won't heal.
Mostly: exposure. You were out there for a while before our chaps
found you."

Al nods and closes his eyes again. He understood about half of
what he heard. The important thing was that he was alive and it was
okay to want to sleep. The nurse knows it's not the time for details.
Rather than overwhelm him, it's better to let him grasp what he can.

"I'm Nurse Kay Davies. You're in the Casualty Clearing Station. You were brought in from a Main Dressing Station yesterday. We are several miles to the rear. I'll be back shortly to check on you.   In the meantime, please rest."

Al nods and lets his body and his mind relax. He falls into a deadening slumber. The sedatives allow him to block out the raw experiences of the past several months. For a few hours, he can let go.

Kay leaves the bedside and steps outside the sprawling tent to steal a scent of fresh air. She breathes deep and closes her eyes. A cold breeze washes over her. As she empties all thoughts from her mind, she lightly fondles the delicate silver cross that hangs from her neck. Part of the left arm is missing. Despite the distortion, the cross dangles perfectly from the chain. The tiny center stone maintains its ballast. The broken cross is Kay's personal crest. She never takes it off. Countless times she has unconsciously reached for it.

It's been a long war for her. Her oldest brother, Hugh, had been an RAF pilot. His Lancaster was brought down during a bombing raid over Germany. Her mother couldn't accept the loss and has been failing steadily for months. Her other brother, Cyril, is on a battlecruiser somewhere with the Royal Navy, probably in the North Sea. Kay keeps their pictures with her as she completes her rounds.

Beside her bed, she has letters from a paratrooper she met while on leave in London. The encounter was brief. No promises made. But their attraction for each other helped normalize life. Awaken the belief that there will be a future. Life does not stop. Life will go on, "just you wait and see," as Vera Lynn's song promises. Contact with her lover is infrequent. She doesn't know if he's dead or alive. She is almost too afraid to care.

When he re-awakens, Al recognizes a familiar sameness. Medical personnel rush to and fro while men lie on cots, either unconscious or chatting with one another. For some, the next stop will be an evacuation hospital. Others are waiting to recuperate so they can be sent back to their units.

Before he has time to put his thoughts in order, Kay Davies re-appears, escorting a surgeon. The RAMC doctor slides next to Al's cot. "I'm Michael Holdsworth, Leftenant. We see from your insignia, you're with your medical corps. Anything seem uncustomary to you?"

"The accents."

Holdsworth grins. "Cousins separated by a common language. No rush to send you back. Let's plan on keeping you here a bit. I'll talk to you before you go. Perhaps we can exchange some observations."

"Right. Trade war stories. Doctor. My Sergeant? Where is he? Was he brought in with me?"

"I'm sorry, Leftenant Jergowsky. We did all we could. I believe his name was Murphy."

Al drops his head and shuts his eyes close. He breathes a deep breath and rubs his forehead. Another loss, another tragedy – but this time it's different…It's Murph.

"We've been together through this mess from the beginning. You will have to forgive me if I …. "

"You needn't explain. We understand."

"Despite everything, you are never prepared to lose some guys. Frank was one of those guys." Al looks up at the two Brits. "We helped each other get through this mess. And now, he's gone."

Holdsworth continues his report. "His leg was smashed when we found him. We rushed him to an Advanced Dressing Station and had to amputate. The ADS doesn't have much in the way of equipment. They had to use an escape saw from one of the airborne chaps to cut off his leg. By the time we received him here, he had lost too much blood."

"I am confident you did all you could, Captain."

Michael Holdsworth taps Al on the shoulder. "I'll see you before you go."

The doctor leaves. Kay Davies stays. She pulls a stool under her and sits next to Al. "Sergeant Murphy asked about you Leftenant. He was as anxious about you as about himself. In fact, strangely, he seemed to worry about all of us."

"That was him."

"He tried to make us laugh at one point. Told us he was from Texas and had a beautiful pair of cowboy boots he couldn't wear anymore. He tried to make it sound like this was his only regret."

Al smiles meekly and recalls the countless remarks and comments that Frank Murphy was known for. "He loved to tell us Texas-size tales about his home." Al pauses. "Murph was wounded around New Year's. He caught some shrapnel during a mortar attack. Got the Purple Heart. The only thing he was worried about was that news of his medal might make the papers back home. He was afraid his mother would learn and worry about him."

Kay was beside Frank Murphy's cot until the end. She couldn't help being moved by this gentle soldier who almost felt guilty by being wounded, not able to assist, and being a burden. One of the last things he said was for Al. "Please tell the Lieutenant I'm sorry."

Kay Davies is arresting. In her mid-twenties, the features of her face and ash-blonde hair give her a particular bearing, a nobility. But what dominates is the weariness. Her pretty grey eyes are expressive, but tired. Her skin is starting to line. Her smiles are rare.

"You know, Leftenant, it seems like I've been doing this forever. And sometimes I try to find something positive. I look, but there just isn't anything there. From time to time I have to force myself. So, I bargain. Too often I find solace when I hear myself say: 'At least their mothers can't see them when they die'."

Al knows the feeling. He looks up at Kay and his expression tells her all she needs.

"Rest now. I'll be back later."

11. Remagen

In the grey morning mist of March 7th, Karl Heinrich Timmerman peers through his field glasses above the Rhine river gorge. A shambolic caravan of trucks, cows, horses, soldiers, and civilians lumber out of the town of Remagen and under the Ludendorff Bridge's castellated arch.

The Ludendorff is a railway bridge built during the First World War. It's the last of the river's 31 bridges to remain standing. While Field Marshal Montgomery meticulously plans Operation Plunder (the plan to cross the Rhine in the north and sweep south), Americans stumble across this prize. A bridgehead on the eastern shore of the Rhine would open a way into the German heartland. A *Wehrmacht* general calls it "the inner door to Germany."

Allied plans for the Rhine crossing were as intense and exhaustive as the D-Day landings: amphibious tanks, searchlight tanks, amphibious carriers for infantry and supplies, river craft, pontoons, airborne tanks, and an unprecedented concentration of artillery. Engineers and planners mine data from specialized hydraulic labs, more than 170 simulation models, and even early Roman accounts of construction projects. Eighty Allied divisions prepare for a final blow.

Stubborn and sometimes fanatical German resistance along the *Westwall* lasted months following the Allied victory at Bastogne. It finally ended at the Saar and Hunsrück. In the early months of 1945, the Allied offensive has been a series of wide-open, fast-moving combat; a breakout from the bitter yard-by-yard slog that marked the fighting since October.

Now, a late thaw has left a filthy coat of slime over the streets and towns in the war zones. Bloated, rotting horses with crushed heads lie aside muddy roads. Dogs lie dead next to human corpses. Gaping craters fill with water and mud. Rubble and the sickly scent of death is everywhere, as is looting by Allied soldiers.

Karl Timmermann is in command of the most advanced column from 27th Armored Infantry Regiment. He was born in Frankfurt, the son of a First World War veteran and his German war bride. Promoted to company commander the night before, he wrote to his wife with the news, but played it down. "There is no glory in war. Maybe those who have never been in battle find certain glory and glamor that doesn't exist…Tell Mom that we will be on the Rhine tomorrow."

Now, he sees before him not just the threshold into inner Germany, but a place in history. Looking down at the intact structure from his perch, one of Timmermann's two scouts is overwhelmed. "Jesus! Look at that…Do you know what the hell river that is?" The short black line on their maps, running from Remagen to the village of Erpel on the opposite shore, represents an earlier end to the war, and the "glory and glamor" that Timmermann scorns.

Supported by a tank battalion, Timmermann and his men prepare to attack Remagen. By early afternoon, they are advancing through the town, vaulting from one building to another. A separate column joins them. Luckily, the resistance is light. They know the bridge is mined. What they don't know is whether it is a trap. How many troops are on the opposite shore? Is the enemy waiting for the Americans to cross before blowing it and stranding the lead column on the eastern side? As these questions hang in the air, the Sherman and Pershing tanks move in to cover Timmermann's company.

"*Sprenge die Brücke! Sprenge die Brücke!*" can be heard over the water. A German captain clasps the keys on a firing switch. He yells to his men, "Open your mouths so it doesn't blow your eardrums!" He turns the keys, but nothing happens. He repeats again and again. Still, no effect. His sergeant makes a desperate dash out onto the bridge. He sprints over 90 yards through gusts of American gun fire to light the primer cord. Bullets from the western shore ping off the iron girders and chase him back to Erpel.

A few moments later, a tremendous thunder rises above the river. The bridge seems to hang in midair. A plume of dust, debris, soot, and smoke churns. When the air and noise settles, the "Ludy" is back atop its stone foundation, abused but unbroken. Was it the use of industrial explosives rather than military grade? Maybe faulty charges or blasting caps? A shell could have severed the demolition cable. Or perhaps – a miracle.

The battalion commander radios Timmermann: "Do you think you can get your company across the bridge?"

"Well, we can try it, Sir."

"Go ahead."

"Yes sir. What if the bridge blows up in my face?"

There's no reply.

Karl and his men begin their race across the Ludendorff, cutting wires and tossing charges into the Rhine. Alexander Drabik, the son of Polish immigrants, commands the leading squad. For a quarter of a mile they dodge heavy machine-gun fire, knowing that the demolition charges might still go off. Through the settling dust and smoke from the explosion at the eastern end, they run down the middle of the bridge, knowing that if they stop, they will be hit. Drabik is the first American across the Rhine. Once in Erpel, he and his men take cover in bomb craters and wait to be reinforced.

While the fighting continues, Eddie Todd's company is sitting in an abandoned school a half-day's ride from Remagen. They have been enjoying a few days off the line. Todd lays back on a cushion of gear and takes in the banter. Some guys joke, others complain. A game of poker breaks out between two Doughs.

"Jersey Jake" Walton deals. "Alright Tex. I'll wager a half pack of cigarettes you're wearing panties and a bra under that gear."

Alvin Cochran inspects his cards like they are his troops. Without looking up he says: "Ya' know pardner, we got a saying back home for cowboys like you. 'All hat and no cattle.' I'll see your chicken-ass pack with a half D-bar."

"Oh yeah. Where can I buy me one of those hats? I wanna be a cowboy. I'll raise you a whole D-bar."

"There's your D-bar and I'll raise with a half-pack of cigs. You don't get it, Slick. It takes more than a hat to be a cowboy."

"I know that, Goober. I'm already an asshole, I just want the hat. Two D-bars. Call."

"Hey! Abbott and Costello, pack it up. We're moving out," orders Pete Sosnowski. That goes for the rest of you comedians. Grab your gear.

"Where to, Sarge?"

"Berlin…genius!"

"Come on, Sarge…Where we goin'?"

"We just heard there's a bridge still standing. Some guys from 9th Armored Division are holding it. We're the cavalry."

The men start grabbing their gear and ammo packs. No one needs to say a word. Everyone knows what this means. There is a sense of collective purpose, an electricity. For all they know, they may be hurling themselves into a killing field – or the history books.

The 311th Regiment of the 78th Infantry Division rides through the night in a convoy of six-by-four trucks. In the darkness of March 8th, at 04:30 hours, they join with a battalion from the 310th. The convoy drives straight through Remagen to the eastern side. Doughs leap from the six-bys through a hail of small arms fire. At the same time the trucks are wheeling around to cross back for reinforcements. A Stuka roars a few feet above the river heading towards the Ludendorff. Antiaircraft guns open up. The pilot is eye-level with the riflemen along the embankment. He drops his bombs, but they explode harmlessly in the water. Almost simultaneously, another dive bomber approaches from the opposite direction. That too fails. It's too late for Germany. The line of US troops swells by the hour. The reinforcements cannot be stopped. Re-capture is no longer possible. The remaining option is delay and retreat.

Over the next two days of combat, the entire 78th crosses to the eastern bank. Yet, the fighting remains desperate. Over a hundred German guns pound the foothold on the eastern shore, including the Mörser Karl siege mortar, fresh from use against the people of Warsaw. Balloons, jet planes, dive bombers, and V-2 rockets are launched from sites in Holland. Joining the cannonade are four hundred Luftwaffe sorties. The sorties are suicide missions. Seven hundred antiaircraft guns, the densest concentration of the war, fill the sky with hard rain.

Clayman, Sosnowski, Todd, Talbot, Sozek, Delaney, Russo, Boyd, Walton, Cochran, Towne, Jergowsky, and the rest of the 311th are the first Allied regiment to cross the Rhine. Given the shortage of infantrymen that month, platoons of "Colored" soldiers answer the call. All cross the bridge at Remagen, bonded by a single purpose.

A delayed justice is reserved for the fifty-three "colored" infantry platoons. They had served as sergeants in the service battalions, as cooks, drivers, dock workers. These troops ceded rank and pay for the nobility of fighting as privates. The resistance to integrate them with combat units came from the highest ranks. They fear that once guns are placed in the hands of Negro troops, they would not hesitate to use them against Whites. But frontline needs overcome rear echelon resistance. One African-American soldier wrote: "Hitler was the one who got us out us out of the white folk's kitchen." Another wrote at the time, "I am an American Negro doing my part for the American government to make the world safe for a democracy I have never known."

They fought bravely and effectively during the breakout. Some *Wehrmacht* and SS troops took particular umbrage from the dishonor of having to fight Negroes. US official recognition for their sacrifice did not come until years later. Despite the success of the integration, it applied to only some infantry battalions, temporarily. A presidential order re-segregated the military in 1948.

By March 17th, the foothold expands over 100 square miles. Enemy artillery fire is stilled. The bridgehead is secure. Only then, the "Ludy" collapses into the Rhine.

The *Führer*, seeking scapegoats and recriminations, subjects four junior officers to a summary court martial. Accused of botching the demolition, the men are tried, convicted, and condemned within thirty minutes. Each man is shot in the back of the head, their last letters to loved ones burned, and their bodies dumped in shallow graves.

Several days after the collapse of the Ludendorff, Supreme Headquarters Allied Expeditionary Force (SHAEF) is exultant, believing the war is over. It is not. American casualties in April 1945 are as heavy as the losses in June 1944. A Texan infantry captain writes; "Mother, you asked me when I was coming home. I don't know. I don't see any end to the war. I can't see what the Germans hope to gain but they aren't giving up." A few weeks later, he is mortally wounded during an ambush inside a town in the Hartz Mountains. A company had earlier secured and declared the area cleared. As he sat calmly in his Jeep, two men stepped out from behind a house and gunned him down with machine pistols.

For every enemy platoon that surrenders, another fights to the death. The Reich's mad psychosis rages on, despite the diminishing rationale and means. A ghoulish, lie-fueled propaganda campaign warns Germans that any capitulation means slavery. There will be mass executions. German women will be herded into Negro brothels. Surrender is treason. In the final days of the Third Reich's fall, Luftwaffe pilots train to conduct suicide missions. Those who refuse to continue the fight drape avenues from streetlamps and telephone poles, garbed with placards labeling them cowards and criminals. Boys in the Hitler Youth detachments break in fear and are shot down by *Wehrmacht* officers. Other children and women toss grenades at allied troops. Some become snipers. If cornered, they are subject to the same battlefield justice as their *Wehrmacht* counterparts. A British POW collapses during a forced march. When a German girl defies the party line and brings him water, an SS man walks behind and shoots them both.

While under fire, American troops struggle with the flow of slave laborers, concentration camp victims, POWs, and local civilians and soldiers who understand the war was over. Germans look desperately for someone to take them prisoner. Slave laborers want to know when they can go home. All are hungry and sickly. Some are at the threshold of death. A "monstrous moving frieze of refugees" were the words used by one witness. GIs who were immigrants or sons of immigrants, and know Polish, German, Russian French, Italian, et al, attempt to establish order. Maintaining order while simultaneously eliminating a fanatical regime in its death throes overextends resources and overwhelms the spirit.

At Morsbach – an ancient city 30 miles east of Cologne – Company G of the 311th finds a "cage" of French, Russian, and Polish prisoners. Not far away, in Konigswinter, Company E encounters an underground airplane parts factory. There, enslaved workers from all over Europe manufactured fuel pumps for Focke-Wulf fighters and heavy military vehicles. In underground tunnels, civilians seek refuge alongside 1,400 slaves. A French boy presses up against a fresh corpse, hoping to draw off the last drafts of warmth.

Tens of thousands of slave laborers swell the cities of Wuppertal and Remscheid. The area is a major industrial region known for textiles, machinery, and chemical production. Its industrial output was critical to the war effort. With the collapse of the Reich, the towns teem with refugees carrying away clothing and food from German warehouses and homes. They bring with them tuberculosis, typhus, and diphtheria. Starvation and rage feeds the looting and reprisals.

12. "God, are you here?"

Al Jergowsky sits in an idle litter Jeep, and digs into his field jacket for a letter he received two weeks ago. Holding it makes him homesick. Regardless of the message, its mere touch brings an odd comfort, just by knowing it's from family. He's read it scores of times, but each time feels like the first. It's a V-gram from his brother-in-law, received weeks after it was posted. Al begins to read it again just as a new delivery of refugees enters the aid station. The brief quiet has exploded into a cantonment of emergencies, traumas, suffering, and wails. They are sick and emaciated. Some have been seriously brutalized. It's back to normal.

Meanwhile, Ed Todd polices a section of nearby woods close to Remscheid. He walks stealthily, ready to use his rifle at the slightest flicker. In the distance, he hears a rustle and the trembling of human-like tones. As he approaches the sounds, they become louder and more convulsive. He recognizes female voices. He relaxes the muscles in his arms and shoulders, but does not lower his rifle. Two girls emerge from behind the trees. They are hysterical and blood-soaked. Their screams become frenzied as they get closer. The sight of a soldier makes them cower. Their desperate need for help collide with fears of more atrocity.

"Alvin!" yells Eddie.

Alvin Cochran and Bernie Schwab rush to assist Todd. The three men stride tentatively with rifles raised. partly out of caution and partly from disbelief and shock.

"What the hell is this? What happened here?" asks Cochran.

"I don't fucking know. Polish? Russian? I can't understand them."

"They aren't Germans," says Schwab.

Schwab puts his gun down and raises his hands, palms up.

One women keeps talking franticly while the other remains dazed and quivering.

"I think they were raped. Before they were tortured, it sounds."

"Tortured?…mutilated more like it."

"Jesus fucking Christ! Did Germans do this? What kind of God-damn animals would do this?"

"Could also be someone from the camps trying to settle a score," says Schwab.

"We gotta get them to the aid station," demands Todd.

"I'll get a medic," Cochran runs off to grab someone.

When the medic pulls aside the blanket to inspect the trauma area, it tears at the woman's flesh and tissue. All she does is whimper and groan more. He applies some peroxide to loosen the dried blood. He draws back her blanket so he can see the extent of her wounds.

"Holy fuck! Someone cut off her breasts!"

Todd and Schwab stare in horror. Cochran repeats the words in disbelief.

"Looks like they could have done this with a bayonet." The medic continues. "I can't do much here. She's got to get treatment. Call for a Jeep. Someone's gotta sit with this one to hold her together. I don't think the other one can manage anymore. And I can't leave the platoon."

Ed Todd nods. "I found them. I'll take them."

Ed climbs in the backseat with the mangled girl. He takes off his field jacket and covers her shoulders. He holds her close, trying to quell her trembling. As they travel over the ruts of the road toward the aid station, Eddie keeps asking: "Enough, enough. When does it become enough?" He can see that under the lacerations and gashes lives a pretty woman. Her eyes are vacant now. Earlier they may have had the look of innocence. What could she have done to deserve this? Did she hide a deserter? Give food to a starving camp escapee? Did she betray someone? Or, was she simply sport for some prison guard or Nazi dead-enders? Ed whispers to himself: "God, are you here?"

They arrive at the aid station. Al Jergowsky comes over to help.

"What's this?"

"The two of them were wandering around in the woods not far from those camps, Sir. We couldn't find out much more, but before they got slashed up, they were probably raped."

Jergowsky's jaw locks with rage while he inspects the wounds.

"The platoon medic guessed whoever did this, probably used a bayonet – the way she's been hacked at."

Jergowsky begins talking procedures aloud. "Looks like they didn't cut any major blood vessels. The best we can do here is give her some I.V. fluids, morphine, irrigate and dress the wounds, dust them with sulfa powder, and maybe give her some penicillin. The skin is gone so the wound will have to granulate in."

Al looks at Todd's blank expression and gives him a quick tutorial as if he were her next of kin. "Granulate: means that it will form its own scar. It will never be normal skin. She would need a major skin graft for that, the type they do for third-degree burns. Of course, that's if she is well nourished enough to survive the healing process."

Jergowsky realizes Ed is too beaten and emotionally flooded for his diagnosis to register. "We'll take it from here. You can get some rest and suck up some fresh air and get some chow – if you can."

Ed nods and walks toward the mess tent. He takes several steps, then like a sudden punch to the gut, he drops to his knees and vomits. The retch mixes with the stains of the girl's blood on his fatigues. He slumps on the nearest supply crate, trying to take deep breaths. He doesn't know how long he's been sitting there when he senses company.

"You alright, soldier?" says Lieutenant Jergowsky

"I'm fine, Sir. Just had a bad moment."

"They've just taken the girl to an evacuation hospital for further treatment. You did all you could. We did, too." Al looks at Todd. Everyone suffers from battle fatigue. How they handle it goes according to each man. "What's your name Corporal?"

"Todd, Sir. Ed Todd"

"I'm Al Jergowsky."

Eddie nods, not knowing whether he has permission to address the officer by his first name.

Al offers Ed a smoke, but Todd politely declines.

"How long you been here?"

"November? December?   Not sure any more Lieutenant."

"I know.   Sometimes it seems I've been here all my life."

"Sir, is it ever going to be normal again? I'm going to live with this day for the rest of my life, aren't I?"

"I've forgotten what normal is, Corporal."

"Ya know, Lieutenant, there were a lot of times I didn't think I knew why we were here or what we were fighting for. But, at least today, I know who."

"Yeah, I understand.   Sometimes I think killing these people is too good for them. If they asked me, I would say strip 'em naked and put them in cages. Then charge people to go see them." Al takes a last drag from his cigarette and crushes it out. "But, that's just me. Is that normal?"

"Would you go through this again, knowing what we're fighting, Lieutenant?"

"The idea is frightening to me. But I honestly have to say 'yes,' gladly. Otherwise, what would be the difference between them and us?"

Ed Todd concurs and bows his head.

Reassured that Ed Todd is going to be alright, Al stands up. "Well. I gotta tend to some things."

"Yeah, I best be getting back to my unit." Ed stands, too. He looks Al Jergowsky in the eye and says: "Thank you Lieutenant. See ya after the war, Sir?"

"You bet."

Al is now free to seek solitude. He finds it on the edge of the encampment against a rotten tree stump. He unfolds the letter once more.

Dearest Brother:

This is a task I've been dreading for the past ten days, but the arrival of your cable reminded me it must be done. Wednesday night (2/14) Pop could not sleep, complaining about difficulty sleeping. Doctor Hankins was called early Thursday and ordered nurses day and night. Oxygen masks and various injections every two hours. He seemed to be doing well Thursday and the following night, but his heart finally stopped when a blood clot caught up with it. We can only be thankful that he was not aware of the seriousness of his condition, and he passed away very peacefully.

The shock has been more than any of us can bear, especially Mom. She suffered an immediate collapse. The best medicine for her would be a visit from you, so we have asked intervention from the Red Cross. Perhaps you can get a furlough during your recuperation.

His funeral was simple and dignified, in keeping with his character and temperament. He's buried at Mount Lebanon next to a friend from the old country. The babies are doing well, and Jay talks about his "Unc Al."

Chin up, and come home soon.

Your brother and friend,

Russ

Al folds the letter and returns it to his pocket. Now, he has to live in a world without his beloved father. The person whose love was unconditional. The person who loved him above all else. Pop was the one who was always there to encourage and support him. Yet, he was discerning enough to understand some trials are personal. And there are times a father needs to step back and allow a son to grow into a man. Where would the son now go to draw on that strength and wisdom? Perhaps, it's not something to expect any more. Rather, the time is for him to teach himself. One day, he will be the one to teach someone else.

Al leans back against the remains of the tree. He looks up at the sky in the vanishing light and closes his eyes.

13. "Enriched by pain"

In a quiet and mostly vacant mess tent, a few GIs and aidmen shuffle back and forth between a coffee urn and the tables. During a welcome lull, the men take the opportunity to rest their minds and heal their nerves. The distant rumble of cannon fire provides a backdrop, but it's mostly unnoticed by the vets. They have come to think of it as an edgy reminder of war and affirmation of the fact they are still alive.

Chaplain Martin Gatti walks in. The deep creases of his face give him the mien of an ancient wise man, but this is only his second tour. His eyes are still youthful and forgiving, despite all they have seen. They land on Al Jergowsky. The two have been beside each other throughout their time at the front. Their New York connection transcends the differences in their faiths and backgrounds. Al often refers to Father Gatti as "Rabbi." Gatti counters with "Saint Al."

Al is sitting by himself, having a coffee and letting his cigarette burn down to his fingers as he reads an issue of *Stars and Stripes*. It is one of his few pastimes when he is not lost in happier times – dreaming about being a boy, again. Growing up in New York and Hoboken. Going to ballgames with his dad and uncles. Watching the Stevens Tech students celebrate the end of exam period with snake dances through the town. Being old enough to go to Frank Sinatra concerts.

"Hey Saint Al, how's it going?" asks the Jesuit priest.

"Same as usual, Rabbi."

"That bad, eh?" responds Gatti. He pulls out the bench opposite his friend.

Al puts down the paper and asks, "I haven't seen you lately. Where have you been hiding, Chaplain?"

"Oh, here and there. In fact, I was at the Passover ceremony last week. It was the first time Passover has been celebrated in this region…this openly."

"What was a nice Fordham boy like you doing at a place like that?"

"Hedging my bets."

After both let out a lax chuckle, Martin continues. "I didn't see you there. Is everything alright?"

"I'm doing well enough. We've talked a lot, Father. You know I took an early retirement from religion."

"Just like that, uh?"

"Oh, I'll never stop being a Jew. Let's say, I just stop going to meetings."

"I know. My club has a lot of inactive members, too."

"They tell us there's no atheists in foxholes, though. So, business may pick-up," Al assures him.

"You can't stay in a foxhole your whole life. You sure nothing's wrong?"

Al takes in a deep breath, and with a low sigh he confesses: "I lost my father, Martin. He had a heart attack when I was missing. He was my best friend. And, I wasn't there. If it had to happen, why did it have to happen before I got home? Another few months…"

"I'm so sorry, Al. I remember you talked about him. There's never any words I can say that will make a difference. Even though I'm in the business."

"Trying counts."

Father Gatti smiles and adds: "To be honest, Greg Towne told me about your father."

"So, you're checking up on me."

Gatti shrugs and smiles.

"I hope you didn't come to quote me scripture," Al warns jokingly.

"You know that's not my style. But actually, I stumbled across some secular text. I thought this Frenchman's writings…humanizing. I understand he was active in *La Résistance*. One passage brought to mind some thoughts and some people. One of them was you."

The chaplain takes out a small book from his jacket and pushes it across the table. "I marked the page."

Al opens it, then as quickly shuts it. "When do you need it back?"

"I don't. It's a gift."

Al nods and says: "Thanks. By the way, it's only fair of me to ask, how are you doing?"

"I'm alright." Gatti pauses, then he, too, sighs. "They are starting to open the camps. These camps were never just a program. They were an entire industry! The barbarisms are unimaginable. I find myself not only helping to bring the prisoners and refugees back to life,

I'm trying help their liberators to cope, too."

"We had a case in here the other day," adds Al. "By the way, that gets me back to my initial question about you. Who is there to give the pastor pastoral care?"

"Ah, that's where faith comes in. I'll probably be staying on for a while. Maybe that's the plan for me."

"God's? or the army's?"

Fr. Gatti lifts a shoulder and raises his eyebrows. "At this point, is there a difference?"

After an hour reviving shared experiences and encounter, navigating through hard stretches, recalling names, the two guys from New York breathe a ragged and exasperated huff. Wistful, contemplative, yearning for some sane undefined conclusion to these past years, Martin Gatti and Al Jergowsky know this part of their lives has ended. There will come times when the struggle is to put aside some memories, imbruing in sorrow and blood. And there will be other occasions when it's a duty to themselves and others…never to forget.

"Good luck, Martin. Keep your sense of humor. I'll be thinking of you. In fact, I'll be thinking of you long after this."

"Same here, Al."

The Jesuit looks down in a reflective moment. When he raises his eyes again he says: "Take care, Al. I'm always here. Come see me if you need anything, or if you're just bored."

"I will."

The two men stand up and shake hands, probably for the last time. Their reunion is gentle but sorrowful. Departure hangs over every life during war, a burdening leitmotif that defines each journey.

Al smiles sadly as he watches Martin leave the tent. He sits silently for a moment and looks down at the book. He runs his hands over the cover and fans the pages. He looks up and stares at the tent opening where his friend passed through. Father Gatti is gone. Al takes the slightly worn book and leans back against a tent pole. An old ticket stub marks a page. He reads:

> …the astonishing or unfortunate thing is that these deprivations bring us the cure at the same time that they give rise to pain. Once we have accepted the fact of loss, we understand the loved one

obstructed a whole corner of the possible, pure now as a sky washed by rain. Freedom emerges from weariness. To be happy is to stop. We are not here to stop. Free, we seek anew enriched by pain. And the perpetual impulse forward always falls back again to gather new strength. The fall is brutal, but we set out again.

Albert Camus

14. In Turmoil, Some Find Repose

Kay Davies is home on leave, trying to reunite with friends and family, to repair. But the healing is hard. Everywhere she is reminded of her brother Hugh. Her mother's condition continues to deteriorate. As a nurse, she has helped so many in this war try to hang on. Now, she has to watch helplessly as her mother lets go.

Her family hasn't heard from Cyril, and she's lost contact with her paratrooper in the 6th Airborne Division. The memories of the men like Frank Murphy preoccupy her. To push them aside makes her doubt her humanity. She is haunted with nightmares that flicker and dissolve. Sleep is illusive.

Tonight, she's staying in London with friends. She promised to go out but she's starting to regret the decision.

There's a knock at the door.

In the doorway is her American friend, Hope Henry, posing like she's on a cover of Collier's. Body turned askance, knee slightly bent, head set back, and hand raised. Hope is also an army nurse. The similarities with Kay end there. While Kay is thoughtful, Hope is impulsive. For Kay, decorum is central. For Hope, it's grandiose. Somehow, they make a perfect match.

Hope's slight frame generates constant energy. No adventure is too outrageous, nor are her comments. It's hard not to notice the auburn-haired twenty-year-old as she flits to and fro, flashing her voluptuous blue eyes, leaving a trail of smiles, laughs, and raised eyebrows.

"Ta-Da! Are you ready Honey?" laughs Hope.

"Naturally," says Kay, dutifully.

"Really? You look as nervous as a cat at a dog show." Hope inspects the digs as she enters.   She turns back. "What's the matter, Kay?"

"What makes you think something's the matter?"

"Well, every time you get anxious I can feel it, especially when you clutch that cross around your neck. You think I don't notice? By the way, I've never asked, but what does that charm mean to you? I've seen you reach for it a thousand times."

Still touching it, Kay breathes in. "My brother Hugh gave it to me just before his last mission. He always had it with him. He kept it in his pocket and took it with him on every flight, except the one."

"Sit, Honey. Let's talk for a while. We are in no rush and the time is good."

Kay looks up from the cross. "Hugh and I were very close, but unlike me he was always taking chances; even as a boy. It used to drive Mum mad. He'd hear it over and over again, how he should behave more sensibly, for the sake of his mother. She dragged him to church every week but he acted like it was a trip to the headmaster. His antics were even hard on me as his younger sister. He never could sit still. Hated taking orders. I suppose we should not have been surprised when we got the news."

"And the cross...?"

"He found it in some rubble after one of the raids. He said the broken left arm represented the unrepentant thief who was crucified next to Christ. Hugh used to joke that he had a fascination with that 'bloke.' But sometimes I think it was more than a pretense. Why he gave it to me before he left, I'll never understand. Except, perhaps, he was feeling something."

Hope is respectfully silent for a while. She takes her friend's hand and pulls her closer on the divan.

"I never met Hugh. But I think I know him. It's funny, when the war came...I welcomed it. It kinda thrilled me. Something big is happening, and I'm going to be part of it, I thought. Even at the time, I wondered if it wasn't an odd reaction. I'll bet Hugh was the same way. I can't explain it, but some of us find in turmoil a sort of...stability. Even, a repose, I guess."

Hope stops to search her thoughts. "I was there on D-Day and at Bastogne. But at Brest, I did something a little crazy. I was assigned to a clearing station in the city. They kept us nurses in the basement of a three-story house for our safety. When the bombarding began, they ordered us to stay in the cellar. That's all I needed to hear. I snuck out, went to the attic. I found a door and climbed on the roof. Standing there in the middle of the bombardment I watched the greatest show I'd ever seen. The lights, the fire, the sounds...I'd never see anything like it – or will again. The minute they told us to stay put, that's when I said, 'No way! No one is going to make me miss out on this show!' If Hugh were me, I bet he would have done the same thing."

Even Hope has her reflective moments. She pauses and wonders about that day.

"I think your brother understood – you can't live your life in fear. Oh, I've seen the same horrors of this war as you. And, I know, you can't ask or expect everyone to be brave. But you have to find your way through it. It's the same in life…for everyone. In the end, it all may be a matter of luck. But until the end, I'm gonna get out of it as much as I can."

"But what about self-preservation?" Kay blurts out. "Don't you have dreams? Don't you want to make plans for the future? Don't you think about anything other than the present?"

"Of course! My plans are to survive this war. And my dream is to be 90 years old throwing out the first pitch on opening day …right at Fenway." She punches the air with a left cross.

Kay looks back with a fond smile. "Hope darling, I truly do love you. But I have no idea what you just said. If it's humanly possible, however, I'm sure you will do it. And I pity this poor chap Fenway, whoever he is."

Hope lifts herself from the sofa and grabs Kay's arm. "Honey we need to talk more often, but right now my plan is to take you down to the USO. We are going to dance, tease the boys a little, then leave them with broken hearts…It's what separates us from the animals."

"Indeed."

"Grab your frock."

The doors of the grand dancehall swing open. The music from the band explodes over the room. For Hope, the scene is a natural habitat. As soon as her feet meet the floor, her hips begin twirling and her shoulders pitch and sway to the beat. Kay follows behind in steady strides. When they land at the bar, several sets of eyes are already fixed on them. Before Hope has time to order a drink, an airman walks up.

"Ma'am, would you like to dance?"

"Sure. Honey. What's your unit?"

The flyboy pulls his head back in surprise, but submits. "The 8th

Air force. Why?"

"The 8th! Oh, my God, I'm not even gonna ask your name. You'll be dead in three weeks!"

"Hope!" cries Kay, like she's trying to housebreak an overly playful pup.

The airman looks at Kay for some sign of explanation. Then he looks back at Hope. "Well, only because you're NOT asking, my name is Art Hammill."

"I like it. Okay, Artie, let's dance. I'll let you lead."

The USO hall is pulsating to the tunes of Benny Goodman, Tommy Dorsey, and Stan Kenton. The music that followed the GIs added an erotic lunacy to their sense of freedom. It emboldened, delighted, and aroused. Nazi Germany banned it. But the British, French, and others of that generation embraced it. It implied a world after the war. Underclasses tired of old men's wars and women who took their men's places, danced with abandon as if they were casting off their subservience.

The Americans stood in stark contrast to British soldiers. The Tommies had no fancy dress uniforms. The years of war, the years of rations, the years of defeats before the victories, make them look spent. The Americans and Canadians appear like titans: well-fed, fitted uniforms, healthy, brash, conquering. A Frenchwoman wrote about her affairs with Americans: "You have liberated me. Now it is up to me to remake my own freedom."

From the corner of her eye, Kay sees an US Army Air Force pilot approach. She can't help admiring his broad shoulders. He has a typical American look. A short, boyish nose, flawless hips and torso, an adorable smile, and perfect American teeth.

"Ma'am, may I have this dance?"

Kay offers her hand as the music slips into something more comfortable. "For All We Know" plays over the room. The frenzy calms as dancers hold each other closely and tenderly, many lost in their own thoughts. Kay rests her head against the flyer's shoulder. She closes her eyes and lets the warmth of his body penetrate her. Sex, in these times is more than a pleasure – it is life affirming. Brief romances create dreams and, often, disenchantment. But, they leave their touch.

Kay and her American continue dancing. She reflexively draws him tighter, as if trying to hold on to her desires. Other yearnings arise, for those she's lost and the lives unfulfilled. Memories make her weep. Finally, the song's parting lyrics speak of sweet sorrow and end with a caveat: "tomorrow may never come, for all we know."

15. Germany, 1945

Millions shuffle across Germany in a kaleidoscope of refugees, former prisoners, and marauding gangs. One observer describes the ferment as, "a scuffing and grating of millions of shoes." Roads congest with farm carts and bakers' wagons pulled by skeletal horses or teams of men and women.

All the nationalities of Europe are on the march, bundles on their backs, plodding along roads between military vehicles and ditches, from the defiled and desperate to the arrogant and absurd. Freed prisoners of war stagger, their bodies covered with scratch marks from clawing at body lice. Rags and toilet paper cover their wounds. SS officers who have stripped their insignias to hide their identities stride haughtily alongside monocled Prussians and Hitler Youth. All they have are their lives and whatever falls in their hands. Some carry coal, wood, or books. Others have bread and wine, even musical instruments. An Australian journalist recalls: "The processions were amazing and ludicrous…heavily salted with suffering." Anonymous shallow graves line the routes between cities. Many simply lie where they die. One man's body is frozen in the position of rubbing his feet; another as he drank from a tire rut.

An American soldier sneers: "There is not a Nazi to be found." Crucifixes suspend over discolored patches of wallpaper where portraits of Hitler once hung. Makeshift white flags or flags of Allied nations drape homes and public buildings. No one knew what was going on in the camps. Everyone was lied to.

While Germans ponder their complexity, some refuse to accept the truth. Too devoted to old lies, they hand themselves over to the darkness. In a home near Heidelberg, GIs find a family of three. A father, mother, and young girl hanged themselves along with the family dog. "The shame of German defeat is too much to bear," reads the suicide note. More than 4,000 suicides occurred in Berlin during the month of April. The SS reported that "the demand for poison, pistols, or other means of ending life is great everywhere."

As the camps are overrun or bombarded, a "liberation complex" pervades Europe. Driven by famishment and revenge, slave laborers burn down their shelters and set upon the German population. They loot and murder. Some cast off their prison rags for business suits and eveningwear taken from local wardrobes. After months of starvation, many meet their end from over-consumption. Shrunken intestines cannot tolerate solid food; their systems rebel. Former slaves accept biscuits from well-meaning Allied troops. When the starving try to slake their thirst, the undigested cookies swell causing stomachs to burst. Many drink themselves to death. A group of crazed Russians die drinking V-2 rocket fuel.

The victors, whelmed in a raging outbreak of looting and revenge, murder their surrendering and wounded enemies. Young Poles and Czechs form militias to commit violent acts of reprisal. They form brutal detention camps crowded with both guilty and guiltless Germans. The popular victims among their own population are the usual suspects – intellectuals, businessmen, and Jews. Poles who protected Jews at the risk of their own lives are warned. Not only will the wrath of God come down upon them for saving the Christ-killers, but the imagined lucre they received as compensation make them targets for plunder. A floodtide of suffering beggars the imagination – even before the discoveries in Ravensbrück, Dachau, and Bergen-Belsen. But events ahead will further test the senses and moral grain.

On the fourth of April, elements of the U.S. 89th Infantry Division enter the remote town of Ohrdruf. Expecting to find a secret Nazi headquarters, they encounter something that causes them to gawk in disbelief. A lieutenant from the 82nd Airborne writes home, "We are united in a bond of shame that we had ever seen such things." Ohrdruf, they discover, is one of more than eighty sub-camps of what became known as Buchenwald. It takes a week for American forces and its able-bodied survivors to secure the entire complex.

In this monstrous network, the majority of inmates are worked to death, starved, or succumb to disease. A further inspection, however, reveals strangling rooms, where prisoners are garroted and their bodies hung on hooks. Priests are crucified upside down. Dissection rooms and operation rooms are part of the medical complex where SS doctors performed ghastly experiments. A grove known as the "singing forest" got its name for the way inmates scream for mercy when dangled from tree limbs with their hands tied behind their back. Buchenwald lies within the environs of the city of Weimar, once the residence of Goethe, Schiller, and Liszt. Now the region is the home of systemic evil.

A paratrooper intones, "It is a defining moment in our lives. Who we are, what we believe in, what we stand for." He is not alone. There will be more such moments.

*****

"Sir, what is this place?" asks the sergeant.

"God only knows, Evans. All I can tell you is the nearest town is called Belsen."

"Captain, what I meant was: What the bleeding hell is this place!"

"I know what you meant.   I know what you meant."

Thirty-six hours earlier, Captain Derrick Sington received orders to accompany an armored column to seize a prison compound near the village of Belsen. The Germans requested a truce to help control a typhus epidemic ravaging the camp and threatening the villages. Until relieved, German and Hungarian guards would maintain order. Separate from the agreement, the war goes on. The tank unit plunges through barrages of mortars, antitank artillery, and ambushes on its way to Belsen. Now, standing before the gates of the camp, he is about to enter a world he never could have imagined. And, like the paratrooper at Buchenwald, it will define his life.

On April 14th, the Oxford-educated former journalist is at the outer perimeter of the compound with his Amplifier Unit: a utility vehicle, an armored car equipped with several loudspeakers, and three interpreters. Sington owes his mastery of German to his father, a descendent of a German-Jewish business family. He cultivated a strong distaste for National Socialism before the war. But soon his anti-Nazi passions will convulse with rage.

He moves his vehicles forward past a forested expanse as British troops set fire to the woods to flush out snipers. Along the roadside are signs alerting, "Danger! Typhus!" Across the entrance is a single pole. Sington sees a group of German officers waiting. A stocky man with a noticeable scar under his left cheek steps forward. He introduces himself as Josef Kramer, *Hauptsturmführer* and Camp Commandant. But to the inmates his title is "The Beast of Belsen." After a short exchange, Kramer takes over the conversation.

"The prison is filled with mostly homosexuals, common criminals, and some political prisoners, *Kapitän*." Kramer notices the loudspeakers and warns. "Oh, and I wouldn't make any public announcements."

"And why would that be?"

"The camp is quiet now. I believe you run the risk of arousing them. And, that would be…unwise."

Before Sington can respond, a staff car rolls up. A British Army major leaps out.

"Why are we stopped here?"

"Sir, this is *Hauptsturmführer* Kramer. He is the camp commandant."

The major sniffs at Kramer with aversion, like he's taking in the foul air. "Get your Amp. Unit moving Captain. We have a camp to liberate."

Sington motions Kramer to jump on the running board. He obeys without protest. The Amp. Unit turns the corner and rolls past a fence. Inside are rows of green wooden huts. The smell intensifies. Deeper into Belsen, the Brits' eyes are stunned by the sight of a simian multitude massing along the wire fencing, skeletons in striped prison rags, and the execrable odor of a monkey house rise to greet them.

One of the translators exclaims, "My God! Their faces look like skulls covered with yellow parchment!" His companion adds, "Right. With two holes for eyes."

Corpses are everywhere. Bodies lie in pits, in and outside of crude huts and hospital buildings, stacked four deep. Some survivors, driven mad with hunger, plunder the remains of the dead. Sington stops to gasp at the sight of a women kneeling down and gnawing on a human thigh bone. Other inmates walk about aimlessly, their expressions vacant with hopelessness.

"What is this place?" Sington keeps repeating, then he nods to one of the translators, "Go ahead."

"Ihr seid frei …Ihr seid frei. You are free…We are the English Army. Be calm. Food and medical help is on the way."

Almost immediately the camp erupts. Shrieking and howling inmates surround the vehicles. The boom and wails of tearful voices drown out loudspeakers. Within several minutes a dozen or more inmates in striped pajamas begin clubbing the crowd with batons and packing case strips. These are the *Kapos* – the inmates assigned by the SS to keep order. The sight of these thugs bludgeoning the mob like prancing zebras stuns the Amplifier Unit detachment. It moves forward.

When they enter the women's camp, a mass of dehumanized souls swarm the vehicles. The prisoners toss leafy sprigs and small branches from the camps birch trees as improvised laurels. Some fall on Kramer who petulantly brushes them aside.

"You must deliver us!...This place is horror!" A girl stretches out her arms and yells, "English! English!...Medicine, medicine." Overwhelmed, she lacks the strength to cry. In the huts behind her are the dying, too weak to lift themselves off the floor. They defecate and die as they sit, lie, and wait for the end. Only a flicker of consciousness remains. Bodies that once held hearts filled with warm aspirations are reduced to polished skeletons, creatures so utterly unreal one of the liberators asks himself, "In the future, will I believe the things I see or will I think I imagined it all?"

The vehicles pull up to the mass of unburied bodies. The colossal heaps of dead are the breaking point – the very apotheosis of evil. The British no longer accept the terms of the truce. The guards are disarmed and Kramer arrested. By the afternoon, the prisoners sack the food stores, and huts with *Wehrmacht* clothing, some to die within hours from over-consumption. The SS barracks and gardens are looted. In the evening, those with enough strength begin to ferret out and kill as many as 150 *Capos*, mostly by pushing them from upper-floor windows. A boy leads Sington to a site where the bodies a several *Capos* lay. The corpses are naked, covered with filth, and their faces unrecognizable. They had been mutilated by the mob until there was nothing left of their heads but a faceless blob.

In his first interrogation as a prisoner, Kramer showed surprising little shame or remorse. In his view, he had carried out his orders faithfully and "had done the best he could." His limited and closed world startle his interviewers. Because he believes he committed no great moral wrong, he remained at the camp – as per his orders.

How could being a loyal soldier conflict with his humanity? His duty as a soldier, a *Hauptsturmführer*, suppressed his individuality and morality.

Josef Kramer was an only child of a middleclass family in Munich. His parents raised him a strict Catholic. Eventually, he became an electrician's apprentice, an accountant, and a department store clerk. These were the highlights of his early years. Most of the time he was unemployed. The rise of the Nazi Party offered him departure from the baseness that normal society had reduced him. The war presented further opportunities.

Kramer entered the Party in 1931, the SS in 1932, where he trained as a prison and concentration camp guard. Promotion was swift. His resume included such addresses as Dachau, Sachsenhausen, Mauthausen, and Auschwitz. In the end his superiors, who once viewed his loyalty commendably, abandoned him. He was the Beast of Belsen – and at the same time, the scapegoat.

"Did you not see these people slowly starving and dying?" asked the prosecutor at his trial.

"Yes – That is to say I did not look at it. But I saw from the daily reports."

"Do you believe in God, *Hauptsturmführer* Kramer?"

"Yes."

16. "How I wish I were like you – a human being"

Richard Barker-Jones decided to leave the Press Center to investigate Bergen-Belsen for himself. Now he is in the heart of the camp, standing before a green barrack. The interior is a cloaca of human rot and degradation. Inside, people are dying before his eyes. He picks his way between the dead. The undulating moans of the sick rise and fall in the gloom. He looks down aghast as a woman clings to his leg. She is too weak to pull herself off the ground, so she defecates at his feet. Liquid yellow bubbles streak her thighs.

More than ten thousand corpses covered Belsen when the British arrived. Fourteen thousand died during the first month after liberation. The cleanup was grueling, sickening, hopeless, soul-devouring. The mixed odor of waste, puss, and sweat is asphyxiating. When off-duty, the medical staff sink into utter intoxication. Without the alcohol for release, they fear they would go stark, barking mad.

Outside, Barker-Jones gasps for fresh air. He makes his way to a nearby bench and vomits. The air is relatively cool and reviving, but the stench of the camp is inevitable. Around him, shaven-headed inmates shuffle about. Their steps tremble as if being pushed. The journalist's shaking hand reaches inside his shirt for a smoke. At once a hand appears offering a lit lighter. Without looking up, Richard dips his cigarette into the flame and takes in a gulp of smoke to smother the fetor.

"Just get here?"

Barker-Jones nods.

"Ghastly…isn't. Excuse me…Alec, Alec Mitchell." He offers his hand.

"Richard Barker-Jones"

"I've been here for three weeks. I couldn't believe what I saw. They seemed to die the moment we touched them."

"You a doctor, then?"

"Actually, still a medical student. I volunteered whilst at university. I imagined it was my last chance to erase the guilt of not having done my bit. I never believed it would be anything like this."

Richard notices Alec's youthful look. It's not the usual gaunt, lined face of someone who has suffered the torment and deprivation of war. Mitchell's hair is thick. His skin is smooth and has color. His eyes are clear.

"I'm here for the BBC. I don't know if I'll be able to find the words."

"You've just quoted everyone at the camp who has written home." Barker-Jones is still shaking, but not as bad as before.

"There are other stories here, you know," says Mitchell. "For example, the German nurses we forced to assist in the recovery. About a dozen arrived from Hamburg the same time I did. The picture of efficiency, they were. Clean uniforms, medical bags…But the sight of them turned this place into bedlam. When the patients realized who they were, they hurled themselves at them with anything they could use as a weapon. Knives, forks, instruments from the dressing tables…the girls' clothes were ripped to shreds from their backs. Those near death couldn't even control their passions. Troops had to be called in to establish order."

Alec breathes out a full breath. Recalling the hellishness of the camp wears on him. But having a chance to talk about it openly offers a sort of release. "Now, I don't know what we would do without these women. They almost put our nurses to shame. But don't tell anyone I said that."

"What made the difference?"

"Shame…I suppose. To a woman, each one set out to earn the respect of the patients and us by devoting themselves to the work. The guilt they bore fed their energy. And their sense of duty as nurses, I imagine."

"Amazingly, there are some bright sparks amidst all this darkness. Alec insists. "I can introduce you."

"I'd like nothing more right now." Barker-Jones eyes a clutch of *Wehrmacht* officers milling around and chatting. Some are wearing medical whites. "What about them? What's their story?"

"I wouldn't bother. They're a whole different story…doctors from a local army hospital. We conscripted them for the camp as well. They strut around like they are above the law. Cheeky bastards."

"Old habits die hard."

"Indeed. You know the old joke: What's the difference between

God and a surgeon? God doesn't think he's a surgeon. Can you imagine a surgeon who is also a party member?"

"Hardly. How do you deal with them?"

"Oh, it's not a problem. Colonel Johnny took matters in his own hands one day."

"Colonel Johnny?" says Richard as he reaches for his notebook

"Colonel James Johnson is the senior medical officer here. Really, for a Scot, he's quite amiable," says Alec with a laugh. "When those little Kaisers refused to muster for parade one morning, he ordered the senior officer hanged. Grabbed the bloody pompous berk by his tunic and had an orderly toss a rope over a tree limb. Johnny had to be restrained. They never carried out the order, but Jerry got the message."

"The Yanks would call Johnson a 'can-do' sort of guy," says Richard.

"The truth is, we'd follow him anywhere. 'A human creature in an army world,' someone said about him. But we all have limits."

"Not hard in a place like this. They seem, somehow, still unbowed, these Fritzes. How do you crush this insane militarism?"

"God knows, but one day a burial detail of Hungarians refused to handle the bodies. Their officer claimed it was a violation of the Geneva Convention. A captain drew his revolver, cocked it, pointed it at the Hungarian's forehead, and when he still refused – shot him dead."

"Any repercussions?" asks Richard, feigning casualness.

"Only for the four other Hungarian guards who tried to rush the captain and his squad. They were shot, too. Everyone ended up in the same pit."

Mitchell flicks his cigarette to the ground. "As for the doctors, oh, they still put on airs. Like to swagger about. But our chaps do a wonderful job of hectoring and taking them down a reasonable notch. The lounge is full of stories at night."

"That is encouraging," says Richard, sounding like an insider.

"There is one you might be interested in talking to, although he is a Bavarian. He was in the Hitler Youth as well, but was never a member of the Party. The others treat him like a little shite, because he's the only one who realizes it's all over. A bit of a loner."

"That might be newsworthy. Can you tell me anything about the others?...What about the locals?"

"On the twenty-fourth the liberation force rounded up the burgomasters. Gave them a tour and had them line the burial pit along with the SS. They put Klein right in the middle of the corpses and took his picture."

"Klein?"

"Fritz Klein – the camp chief medical officer. Now the 'mad doctor of Belsen,' after a week of burying bodies. He tried to lie his way through his interrogation, but a Polish girl who was the translator called him out. After some roughing up he eventually came clean."

"And the general population? What did you do with them?"

"Well, we forced the townspeople to work on the initial cleanup. Amazingly, 'nobody knew these things were going on'...despite everything, the traffic, warnings of disease, the odor."

"A common refrain in Germany these days."

"They are paying, believe me," says Mitchell, somberly. "Someone authorized the expulsion of residents from the town of Bergen, and then permitted camp inmates to loot the houses and buildings. Much of the town was set on fire."

Richard takes a deep breath, "I must say, there is an emotional release watching the Germans being bullied, operatic almost...seeing these people trying to maintain their dignity and pride whilst being tormented by howls...rocks...bayonets."

Alec nods. "The SS were made to handle the dead without gloves. Several have already died of typhus. Things will change once the death rate becomes unacceptable. Not sure when that will be."

"What about those 'bright sparks' you mentioned?"

"Ah, a group of Polish girls. Medical graduates of Warsaw University. They somehow managed to hold on to their...nobility – in spite of all this. Knowing them has been quite humbling. You can meet them tomorrow if you want."

"I do."

The next day, Mitchell and Barker-Jones make their way to the women's barracks. "All of them speak some level of English, so you won't need an interpreter."

The two men enter a small hut. It's crude, but clean. There are even a few sprigs of spring buds. The women stand up as Mitchell and Barker-Jones walk in. The sight of Alec brings smiles around the room. They are a little older. They seem to treat him like a brother.

"Richard, may I present Ewa, Hedzia, Basia, and Zosia. Ladies, this is Richard Barker-Jones. He's reporting for the BBC."

Richard returns the smiles and gives a respectful bow of his head. "Here is my press card."

Basia waves it off. "No need. You are Alec's friend. You are welcome here."

"You are medical students from Warsaw, I understand."

"All, except Riva."

"Riva? That's not a Polish name, is it?"

"No. Riva is Jewish - and a saint. You will meet her."

Alec takes his leave. The interviews gone on for more than two hours. The women alternately sit down with Richard and leave the hut to work. Hedzia speaks English best and is most engaging. She comes from an upper-middle class family in Warsaw. Her father was a professor at the university. All were part of the Home Army. When the surrender came, they were given prisoner-of-war status but sent to Bergen-Belsen. Hedzia's boyfriend escaped and continued fighting with a partisan group. They haven't seen each other since. That was more than seven months ago. The last she heard he was still alive. Hope gives her the drive to go on.

Toward the end of the interview, Richard asks, "Can you place your finger ...er, identify the single reason why you are still alive?"

"Luck is always a factor – whether at war or at peace. But for me, it is the hope that love brings. It is such a power. You never fully appreciate its strength. I draw from it every day. I want to survive – for him, for Marek. To be together again. We were separated at the surrender of Armia Krajowa. I haven't seen him since, but if you still have dreams, there is nothing in your way. You will survive, you will overcome, it doesn't matter what happens. In this way, I consider myself lucky...very lucky."

With her fearless eyes, Hedzia stares into Richard's. "Let me leave you with one thought. If there is anything I've learned: it is that, it is not enough to live, you have to have something to live for."

Richard nods, but is not sure what to say.

"You should talk to Riva," Hedzia goes on. "She is one who has lost everything. Yet, she manages to find a reason to hope, somehow. After her husband and son were taken from her at Auschwitz, she continued on. She worked at the camp hospital despite not having any medical training. Caring for the sick and dying renewed her will to go on. She has an aspect about her that these monsters somehow respect. I saw her manipulate SS guards into providing some food for a little Dutch child. Her smile worked magic on these beasts, as did her courage."

"I look forward to meeting Riva. Any final thoughts before I let you go back to work?"

Hedzia sighs as she looks down at the floor. When she looks up, she adds: "Either you are a survivor or you are not. We all have a survivor instinct inside us. It's an internal voice, not an intellect or some light of reason. It's a different understanding. You embrace it because it tells you what to do. And you do it without thinking. Those who don't heed the voice will be victims."

"Thank you. I learned so much," Richard confesses. "So very much."

Barton-Jones is in a momentary trance. The emotions have battered and drained him, but his professionalism has held. He reaches inside his pocket and pulls out his notebook, again. As he scribbles some more words, he says; "Forgive me. I neglected to ask one final question. I tend to collect the responses in a special folder I keep for my notes"

Hedzia smiles.

"Is there a certain moment burnt into your memory that characterizes or represents these past years? What would you say if anyone asks you, 'Give me one story that reveals your life during this time.' — Is there such a story?"

She looks to the ground, again, searching for an answer. But she already knows what that story is. She thinks about it every day since it happened.

"The Germans destroyed all camp records. We had to recreate them by interviewing the inmates. I was helping with the patients in the hospital. Some of them were within days of their last breath. A girl in her early twenties was dying of typhus. I was as gentle with her as I could. I asked her name, and if possible, where was she from. She didn't seem to understand. Finally, she said: 'Me…no name. I am a number, a Jew. You understand? I am a dog.' I waited for her to gather her strength. When she looked up at me, she seemed to be looking at the other side. I have seen that look so many times. Her last words to me were: 'How I wish I were like you – a human being.' She was gone the next day. Can you imagine those being one's last thoughts?"

A fitting silence follows. Both Hedzia and Richard rise. They hug each other for a moment. When they let go, she gently strokes his face. His eyes begin to well up. They smile at one another and return to the world.

17. Reunions

Kay Davies sits at the bedside of a young girl. As she strokes her thin hair, she softly asks, "Please dear, tell me about your friends... about your dolls...pets...What did your mother call you when she was trying to find you?"

The girl looks up. "Hannah. She used to call me Hannah."

Kay smiles gently and kisses the girl's hand. She motions one of the German nurses to administer a dose of vitamin C. When the nurse approaches with the syringe, Hannah erupts in terror. Two English nurses rush to help.

The uproar attracts Dr. Hadassah Bloch. Bloch is a Polish Jew who was educated in France. The camp inmates have come to love and trust her. A senior British military officer described her as "the personification of the triumph of good over evil."

"There, there, child...it's alright. I am here. We need to get you better."

She takes the hypodermic and searches the girl's arm for a usable vein. Kay kneels on the opposite side of the bed stroking her head.

"There. All done. Now we are going to give you a pill to help you sleep. You need your rest."

Bloch rises and nods to Kay. Kay places a few thin strands of hair off to the side and follows the doctor.

"Kay, despite all you have seen, you don't truly understand. This girl reacted to the sight of the needle because the monsters at Auschwitz would inject benzene into prisoners."

"For what purpose? How in God's name..."

"So they would burn faster in the crematoria."

"My God!" Kay hisses. "I thought I had seen all the corporal mess there was to see...but this! I..."

"I know. I know. But I'm afraid you'll find no sympathy here... Nor gratitude, at this point. I've helped to save more souls by bullying them back to life than I would admit. This place is about survival. You'll see I treat my staff with the same discipline. But I'm trying to get them through this period of their lives as well. Here, everyone is a victim – inmates and liberators."

Kay blows out sharply.

"I lost everyone at Auschwitz. Then Mengele sent me to Bergen-Belsen. You will see a hint of the outrage and death I saw at Auschwitz, but you can't let it break your spirit. Before every ordeal, every exposure to the madness, if you don't stay mentally whole and calm – you'll do no good here. Later, there will be time enough to cry."

"You'll find no complaints here."

"Good."

The two women walk past the rows of cots. From their beds, patients mumble their pleas and prayers. Some want to know what happened to loved ones. Others ask if they will ever look normal again. Then there are those who feel the need to speak of their own tragedy.

"My husband was flogged to death in front of me." "My child was ripped from my arms. I never saw him again." "My parents were gassed." "*Herr Doktor, bitte schön, Herr Doktor…*"

Patients clench at their clothes, pleading with them to stay. Hadassah whispers quietly to Kay: "As sad as it is, it is an improvement: earlier, all they could do was breakdown and cry."

The two women pause at the exit. Hadassah takes in a moment to survey the camp area.

"It's soul searing. I worry if the rest of the world will ever fully understand what was committed? And, if it does, will it want to remember?"

Then she turns in the direction of the nearest barrack, with an abrupt announcement: "I'm off."

Kay's hand moves to her beating heart and clutches at her one-armed cross. She sometimes wonders if she has the mental armor to function at Bergen-Belsen. But she has learned doubting oneself during war has fateful consequences. When the call for volunteers had come, her arm went up without hesitation. Her brother Cyril had gone home to bury his mother. He remains to help his father cope and recover their lost time together. Kay didn't see the point of returning home, yet. What more could she offer? And wouldn't she be more valuable on the continent? Her English paratrooper and American flyer are gone.

She takes a letter from her tunic. Happily, the letter is from Hope. It includes an informal wedding announcement. The pilot, whom she guaranteed wouldn't last three weeks, made it back. He asked her to marry him. "The next time you see me, I will be Mrs. Hope Hammill. And the best thing is, I can keep my monogram. I won't need new luggage!"

Kay's thoughts of Hope not only bring a smile, but helps remind her of possibilities. People will go on, live their lives, irrepressibly – without a thought about disaster, loss, or defeat. As Hadassah told her, "It's all about survival." Her friend Hope is a survivor. Kay wonders about herself. Is there a secret to it?

Before she can answer those questions, a US Army Jeep rolls by. She's distracted by the curious sight of two Americans. This is a British Army sector and the Yanks have their own problems. There is familiarity about one of the men. "But that's impossible."

The Americans approach a makeshift reception area. A startled Royal Army Medical Corps orderly notices the medical patches on their uniforms.

"Can I help you, gentlemen?"

"Yes," says the lieutenant. "I'm looking for a Riva Rosenthal." He pulls a letter out of his shirt pocket to check the spelling. "She may be registered as Riva Dzierzgowska-Rosenthal; D-Z-I-E-R-Z-G-O-W-S-K-A."

A nurse overhears. "I know Riva. I can take you to her. My name is Zosia."

"Al Jergowsky. And this is Captain Greg Towne." Towne touches the tip of his garrison cap in a casual salute.

She smiles. "I am going there now. Please let me take you."

"If it's no problem."

"No, not at all." She blushes. "You are the first Americans I've ever seen; except in the movies."

"Well then, you are probably a bit disappointed," laughs Greg. He turns to Al and says, "I'll wait for you here. If she or you need anything, I'll be in the building. Maybe I can help these guys out as long as I'm here."

Al nods. It was Greg Towne who offered to make the long ride with Al to Belsen. He didn't want to see his friend make this trip by himself. They have been through enough together. Why stop now just because the war is over?

On their way, Al and Zosia pass through the stench of death and decay. Waiflike camp inmates, with grotesque forms and movements, totter past.

Al and his escort move on. The battlefield scenes of human parts, disfigured faces of the dead and their deathly smiles are the stuff of nightmares. But, the horrendous wounds, burns, severed limbs, collapsed organs – all manner of butchery wrought by war doesn't compare with the carnage of the camps. It is a different kind of slaughter – a separate strain of dehumanization is on parade here.

"The cleanup would have been more complete by now if we had not so many fatalities during the initial weeks of the recovery," Zosia explains with more casualness than Al is ready for.

The two of them walk without much talk. At the shack where Zosia lives with four companions, she gestures toward a slight figure of a woman on a bench. She looks with grey eyes into Al's.

"There is Riva. I'm glad to have met you Lieutenant. Be well, and may God bless you."

"Thank you, Zosia. May He bless you, too."

Al turns back to the woman on the bench. Despite the month of May, the harsh winter of 1945 is stubborn. A stiff breeze carries the cool air through the buildings and the rags of clothing. Riva sits with her legs crossed and an elbow resting on her knee. She holds a cigarette pinched between her thumb and index finger. A fragment of an army blanket is around her shoulders. The rest of her clothes are Red Cross donations. Despite exhaustion, she maintains a distinctive bearing. A chilly elegance cloaks her. The ugliness of her surroundings, of her past, seem to have lost their control.

Al heads towards her. Her hair is greyed, but not matted or uneven like many. She is lean, but not skeletal. Her face is thin, but not sunken.

"Excuse me. Are you Riva?" asks Al in pidgin Yiddish.

"Yes."

"Riva Dzierzgowska?"

"Yes. That was my name."

"My name is Al Jergowsky."

She does not change expression even though she can feel her heart begin to race. This is not just another soldier conducting camp business. His uniform is different. She can see there is something strangely familiar about him. But, she cannot explain it. When she realizes he is wearing American insignia, Riva offers, "I can speak English if that is better for you."

Al smiles gratefully and continues in English. "Your father was Aron and your mother's name was Kara? Is that so?"

Riva, stunned, nods. "Yes, those were my parents' names!"

"They were my aunt and uncle. I am your cousin."

"My Father was Dawid, your father's brother. We left Poland when I was four."

"Yes, Yes. My parents spoke of your father. He had two children. Are you the one they called Adek?"

"Yes. My name was Abram. But I've been Al for a long time."

"May I sit down?"

There is a long silence as Riva and Al look for any resemblance that connects them. Each try to understand and reflect on the moment. The sense of fatefulness is undeniable. Riva and Al's lives are very opposite, yet, so intertwined. The irony is uncomfortable at first. Hesitantly, a conversation evolves. There are awkward pauses. But once they get past the initial shudder, the two begin to talk more openly. They shift between Yiddish and English. Smatterings of French help to add nuance. A conversation flows about their homes and what they know of the family history. The difficult parts are glossed over or avoided completely. This is not the time to speak of such things. Those events speak for themselves. Instead, they fill each other in on details and stories about the family tree and diaspora. Who is from where? Who went where? What was the news about them? They do not dwell on the tragedies. Rather, they try to speak in the present as much as they can. Gradually, they form a complicated and delicate bond.

As the sun begins to set, Riva asks, "Adek, do you know what the root word of our surname means in Old Polish?"

Al's smile brims now. "No, tell me."

"It means 'to tear.' But not as in to rip or cut, but to tear away, say from a bad situation. As to tear free."

There is a pause and sad smiles. The conversation grows quieter. Al looks for a way to restart. "You know, back in New York they are beginning the process to sponsor your citizenship. You will be coming to America."

"Yes. I've been in contact with your family through the Red Cross. The letters have come, but I've learned to control expectations. So, if I am to become an American – tell me, what will that be like?"

Al takes a moment to think, and then tells her, "Well, I had a professor at the university who maybe said it best: 'America is more than just a country, or a nation of a specific people. It's an experiment.' I think the experiment will still be going by the time you get there."

Riva nods approvingly. "My father loved experiments. He was a researcher at heart. He had a favorite expression, in Russian: *Pozhivom, povidem*: 'We will live, and we will see.' It was his punctuation for every unanswerable question. He told me the Russians like to end their meetings with that exact phrase."

Riva suddenly looks up at a familiar face approaching them.

"Kay! How fortunate! Can I introduce you to my cousin, Lieutenant Al Jergowsky, United States Army," she says, proudly.

"We already know each other, the Lieutenant and I."

Riva looks confused. Al stands up immediately dumfounded.

"My God! …Kay! …You!"

"And in all places," she adds, humorlessly.

"Indeed. In all places."

Kay explains to Riva without taking her eyes off Al. "The lieutenant was a patient of mine – during the counteroffensive." She continues more quietly. "I didn't recognize you at first. I, therefore, decided to speak with Captain Towne, whom you left stranded at the Administration headquarters. It was too providential for me not to see you before you leave."

"I'm so glad you did."

"By the way, both of you are invited to dine at the 'officer's mess' tonight."

Al can see Riva droop. "You go Adek. It's been a long day. I need my rest."

Al is disappointed, but does not want to pressure her. "I'll be right along Kay. I just want to say goodbye to Riva."

"You two take your time. I'll see you at mess."

Al watches Kay turn and leave. He never realized until now how much he has thought of her since they met in the field hospital. Seeing her again is reviving and bittersweet. He cannot dismiss his feeling for her.

Al turns back to Riva and sits down opposite her, again. "Is something wrong?"

"No, no. Kay is fine, but you don't understand. I am still an inmate here."

"And…?"

"The British expected to find grateful victims, but we disappointed them. There are no rose petals to toss at their feet. Instead, there are brawls, stealing, profiteering in the camp. To be dominant is to survive. To them, we are beings from the other side. The British sometimes feel like zookeepers, or like explorers from a higher civilization, here to assist and evaluate people in a region at the end of the world."

"You feel patronized?"

"I feel comfortable with my own kind. Don't pity me. It's hard to understand, but inside that hut there is an unspoken love and acceptance I won't find anywhere else. There is no need to talk when you already know someone's thoughts."

"Is there anything you need? If there is, please let me help."

"No, no. You have done so much by just coming here. Thank you."

Al studies her slight frame and sorrowing blue eyes. "Will you be alright?"

Riva touches his arm and softly smiles: "After this, nothing can ever happen to me."

For only the second time in their lives, they gently hug each other. "Here's my contact information if you need me, Riva. The Army will make sure I get your message."

One last smile, and Al turns to leave.

As he walks away, Riva can almost see Belsen retreating into the past. The future is coming. She watches Al's outline fading into the distance.

Finally, she sighs, "Although I am no longer afraid of dying, will I ever overcome the fear of living?" Her father's voice echoes in her mind: "We will live, and we will see."

Sitting there alone…It's then, at last, that Riva finds somewhere within herself the permission, the freedom, and courage to weep.

.

18. Horizons

Klaus Haas returns the press credentials. He looks over Barker-Jones with worn eyes and envies Richard's wholesome, clean looks, and state of health. In contrast, Haas's *Wehrmacht* uniform hangs off his shrunken frame. His face is drawn and creased. His previous thick hair is thinning. The hard jaw line is beginning to sag. Painfully, Haas recognizes in the Englishman a bearing he once held and now has all but withered away.

"Dr. Haas, I understand you are the only member of German staff here who was never a member of the National Socialist Workers' Party."

"Yes, that is true."

"Although you were a member of the Hitler Youth. You even appeared in one of Leni Riefenstahl's films."

"Yes. 'Victory of the Faith'. I was a mere boy," he pleas. "I was still a Gymnasium student. The Hitler Youth was appealing then. It was hiking, camping, sports. There was weapons training, too. But, I somewhat enjoyed that, I must admit. However, my interest ended early."

"So, why was it you never joined the party proper?"

"A general distain for politics. Once the indoctrination started, I began losing enthusiasm. I was already struggling with my religious faith as a young man. Why would I want to take on another?" Haas pauses. "By the way, your German is very good. Are either of your parents German?"

"Thank you, no…no. I studied at university and worked at the Berlin office for two years."

"I see." Haas nods and continues. "I was attracted to politics at first, but was never completely comfortable with these movements. Bavaria, where I'm from, was susceptible to revolutionary movements. You probably know that."

"Right. The failed Munich Soviet Republic in 1919 though short, was brutal. And, that must have reinforced the independent streak among Bavarian Catholics."

With an agreeable tone, Haas smiles and nods, "I see you know your history, or at least, have done your homework."

Haas resumes his commentary. "I was too young of course at the time, but the sting left a mark. Particularly on people like my parents who were devout Catholics. Atheism never was a good doctrine for attracting converts in places where I come from."

"So, when did your scorn of politics begin?"

"I began wavering a few years out of university. The militarism and anti-intellectualism did not suit me. I was looking for answers. All religion and politics offered was miracle, mystery, conspiracy, and authority. I went on to other pursuits."

"You make it sound like you were merely distracted...whilst the rest of Germany was at the barricades. Was it so easy?"

"No, it wasn't.   There was pressure to join. But, I refused to hand over my freedom of thought. In the end, I resisted." He stares at the floor and sighs. "Maybe it was a voice inside me that simply said: 'This is horribly wrong. This will not end well'." He shakes his head with disgust and incredulity.

"Interesting you should say that...about the voice. Another person told me something similar." Richard continues writing in his notebook.

"The blind fanaticism." Haas lifts his head. "You are familiar with Clausewitz's 'Theory of War'? That 'war is a continuation of politics by other means'?"

"Of course," replies Barker-Jones with a shrug.

"Well, what happens when politics becomes war – by other means. That transfiguration attracts fanaticism. And, I didn't have the proper stomach for it." Klaus shifts uneasily in his chair. "Pardon me, but could I trouble you for a cigarette?"

"Certainly, forgive me for not offering." Haas inhales over the flame of Richard's lighter.

"Ah. It's amazing what a luxury this has become. You know, Hitler tried to ban smoking. He utterly despised it. But the ban failed. Even fanaticism has its limits of what it will tolerate in the name of the *Vaterland.*"

"How do your comrades, here, regard your interpretation of history?"

Haas smirks.   "With contempt, naturally. Their damn militarism sustains their feelings of superiority. And I've soiled their honor by refusing to show the British how a German soldier behaves even in defeat."

"Yes, so I have heard."

"Here's a hint. I have been told that the Americans now ban German insignias or signs of rank. Saluting German officers is also prohibited. In the POW camps, the military world has come crashing down." Klaus adds with a sinister grin, "These martinets also have to deal with the indignation of taking orders from Negro guards."

Barker-Jones continues writing. "One last question. How did a civilization that produced Schiller, Schopenhauer, Handel descend into such madness? What does it say about Germany? The German people? Why a land of such contradictions?"

Haas looks over at Richard. An odd simper cuts across his face. "Do you think we Germans are really that different than you British? Or the Americans? No, my dear Barker-Jones. We are all made of the same atoms. It starts with a single lie. In our case, the lie was Germany did not lose the war. We were betrayed at Versailles by the elite, the socialists, the international bankers, and, of course, the Jews. A lie that everyone wanted to believe in, no matter how absurd or irrational. It explained away our failures and justified our grievances – personal as well as national. These primal emotions crushed everything in their path. Norms, facts, reason – none of that mattered anymore. *Populus vult decipi, ergo decipiatur.*"

"The people want to be deceived, therefore let them be deceived," translates Barker-Jones.

"I see you know your Latin. But, do you know where the quote is from? From a 16th Century Pope. Pope Paul IV – the very pope who ordered the creation of the first Jewish ghetto."

Richard turns the interview back to asking questions. "So, one man with a drum and the proper drumbeat is all there is to it?"

"Oh no. It's quite more complicated than that. Hitler learned his lessons at the *Bürgerbräukeller.*"

"The Munich beerhall putsch."

"He understood he couldn't overthrow a modern state with a violent mob of outsiders. He needed to work within the system. He recruited from the army, the police. Eventually the industrialists stood with him. He ran the elections. Infiltrated crucial institutions. The Parliament was at constant impasse. All this he did before he had a majority." Haas inhales another puff of smoke. "You must constantly nurture your democracy my friend, otherwise, the weeds will choke the life out of it."

"And the war?"

"Even as a mere captain it wasn't hard to understand how things were going once the war was being lost. The latrine grapevine is the government propaganda antitoxin. Hitler surrounded himself with ambitious men posing as sycophants – eager to play along with the comedy. But, instead, he played them. Set them against one another when he wasn't killing them off. He brought the chaos to the war effort. In the end, it was the Anglo-American alliance that was centralized, unified, and coordinated. British discipline and American audacity was more than a match for the Axis…I was in the Ardennes – and at Monte Casino before that."

Haas slumps in his seat. Reliving the disastrous lost years is tiring. He moans, "Now, the German people will be paying for generations. All because of one man's madness."

"Well, *Kapitän*, you have given me an unsettling epilogue for my reporter's notebook."

Klaus looks up at Richard and drones: "It was my pleasure."

"This has been enlightening, to say the least. Thankyou."

"Not at all, Mr. Barker-Jones. Allow me to walk you out."

The two men raise themselves from their chairs and walk together into the yard outside the building.

Before departing, Haas looks at Barker-Jones and sheepishly asks, "If I'm not imposing may I…"

"Certainly. Here. Take the whole pack. I have plenty. Compliments of Bernard Law Montgomery."

"In truth! How so?"

"Monty likes to buy journalists' love by handing out cigarette packs from his car. He has a caravan of goods with him just for that purpose."

"Ah, so at least they are not stolen, eh?" says Haas feigning moral rectitude.

"But they are – by the Field Marshall."

A final sarcastic grin: "*Danke*. Mr. Barker-Jones."

"*Abschied, Doktor.*"

As Richard disappears, Haas lights up another cigarette. He leans against the side of the building and lets his thoughts drift.

His mind's eye inevitably settles on the German child POWs – the 12 to 14-year olds who were either in the *Volkssturm* or who were manning the anti-aircraft flak guns. These urchins volunteered to fight for the *Führer* in the final hour of a lost cause. Stuck in uniforms too big for them and sent to the front, they were slaughtered on the battlefield. Some who were too frightened or refused to fight were summarily executed by party activists.

Those who were able to surrender were the first to die in the prison camps. These scared little boys survived the war only to perish from starvation. Haas witnessed their bloated stomachs, their running sores, the discoloration of the skin and felt the gnarling of their bones. Sobbing and hallucinating, these children succumbed, finally. Their bodies blanketed under a choir of camp tents. Klaus shudders with rage how some *Wehrmacht* officers took umbrage whenever these children received any special treatment. The absurd grandeur of these men who surrendered their arms and their country, but not their sense of entitlement.

Klaus Haas stares vacantly at the ground beneath his boots. He cannot help ruing the war. The *Wehrmacht* underestimated the US citizen soldier. The casual relationship between American officers and the men would result in disobedience, slowness of execution, lack of cohesion, it was believed. Often, it did. But, ultimately, the institution held against the Prussian traditions of the military class.

There were the defeats at Sbeitla and Kasserine Pass. In the Ardennes, whole divisions broke and ran. The dismal failures at Hürtgen Forest exposed the ineptness of the U.S. command. Despite the foibles of missed opportunities, waste of life, carelessness, and categorical stupidity, one Frenchman captured the conflict in Europe with a simple précis. "The Americans waged war as if they were digging the Panama Canal right through the German Army." Thirteen U.S. divisions in Europe suffered 100% casualties or more. Five divisions surpassed 200%. And yet, the Americans always believed they would win.

Klaus finishes his smoke. He rips what's left of the cigarette butt and tosses the shreds into the air. The breeze catches the ash and scraps and scatters them. He stares vainly into nowhere. He thinks about his future and the future of Germany and whispers, "What now?"

Once back at the Press Center, Barker-Jones is making the latest comments in his reporter's notebook.

> The Golgotha of Bergen-Belsen is beyond description. A hellish phantasmagoria that repulses the senses. Yet, horrid as are the sights, sounds, and odors, I cannot turn away. It is not the revulsion that attracts me. It's the fascination with the truth. No matter how sickening, my commitment to history compels me to breathe the foul air, gaze at the twisted images, and touch the sores.

> The array of interviews is quite catholic in experience and circumstances. The gallery includes portraitures of monsters and saints, cynics, satraps, and everything in between. Whether they are victors or vanquished, everyone in their own way is a victim.

> There are the questions for the future.   I wonder if the end of the war means the era of European supremacy is at end as well. Is the US policy of isolationism gone, too? Surely, the post-war era will be a tremendous catalyst for change. But, how will that shape us? What will the coming balance of power be? Will we make the same mistakes, or invent new ones? Oddly, as I reflect on these things I keep going back to the subtle warnings of a US president. John Adams once said: "Power always thinks it has a great soul."

> Other great questions haunt me. What part of history will Germany and the rest of the world remember? What facts will be revised? What truths will be willfully forgotten? In the tribute of tears, will there be more casualties among the unremembered, the abandoned, and the powerless? If we dare ignore the full truth, I cannot help but fear that a century of prayers will not save us from ourselves!

Richard Barker-Jones closes his notebook. He reaches for another cigarette, lights up, and shuts his eyes.

Inside the officers' mess the mood is somber but lax. Shop talk is mostly relegated to the most critical items. Some men trade stories about their latest medical case. Gradually, the conversations shift to grapevine rumors and war news. Several rounds of hard drinking loosen tongues. Light banter and smiles leaven the subdued room.

By the time Al arrives, the mood is almost jolly.

Al scans the tables for any sight of Kay or Greg. Towne's mitt of a hand rises above the sea of heads to wave him over. Through the clutter, he sees Kay's smile. Greg and she have save him a seat between them.

"Have I missed anything?"

"Only Greg's details of how he and you won the war singlehanded," taunts Kay timidly.

"Untrue!" protests Towne as he pours Al a drink. "She never let me go into the details."

Kay lifts her glass and says, "Here's to meeting you, Captain; and to seeing you again, Al."

As the drinking intensifies during dinner, so the volume. Al understands why Riva feels uncomfortable with these invitations. At best, conversations devolved into military drivel. At worst, topics could become salty.

An hour passes, and Greg, Kay, and Al know it's time to move on.

Kay is the first to acknowledge the hour. "Well, the dinner seems to have turned into a party, and I have got another day tomorrow."

Greg agrees. "We still have the trip ahead of us." He begins to push away from the table. "Let me say a few goodbyes and I'll meet you at the Jeep" After a warm goodbye to Kay, Greg starts to circulate the room for the last time.

"I'll walk you back to your building?"

As they walk, Kay and Al can feel the air become warmer. Spring will not be denied. The scant fragrance from a flourish of blossoms rises in the air.

"So, how soon will you be going home?" Kay finally asks.

"Not long. I have enough points."

"And then what?"

Al glances off in the distance and shrugs. "Who knows. I learned a new adage today: 'We will live and we will see'."

"Mmm…" Kay utters and abruptly asks, "Are you married Al?"

"No, Kay. I'm not married." He pauses before continuing. "But, …I have a son."

The two stop and turn to look directly in each other's eyes.

Al adds. "And he has a mother."

"I see."

"He has a mother, a name, and he's even baptized."

"Baptized?" notes Kay.

"Helen is Catholic."

She smiles fondly and tells Al. "I think he's a rather lucky boy. He will be brought up by a capital father."

They walk the last few steps to the entrance of the barrack. Kay and Al turn and embrace. They hold on to one another and feel the warmth. Both want to create a memory each can hold on to – a moment that is full of potential but still innocent.

They separate, and Al stays and watches Kay fade into the shadows. Will this be their last time together?

Once inside, Kay prepares for bed. She sits on the edge of her cot. Kay has survived the tragedies of love and war. The world does not control her as it once did. When she arrived at Belsen, she never pulled back. She made a point of seeing the worst conditions and treating the most appalling cases. She did the work when others flinched. Not due to a morbid attraction, but because she felt it a duty to become a witness to the horror and in some small way, attempt to undo it. The unbroken and generous spirit that Hadassah Bloch demanded was alive in her. The past years made her less afraid to take risks. She emerged from the revulsion of war not merely a stronger person, but a person of her time.

She breathes in and unclasps Hugh's broken cross. It drops into the cup of her hand. Kay puts it away in her charm box with her other valuables. It's the first time the necklace has not hung from her throat since the day she put it on.

She closes the draw and shifts under covers. She picks up a book by her bed. Before turning out the light Kay reads a favorite passage:

> Freedom emerges from weariness. To be happy is to stop. We are not here to stop. Free, we seek anew enriched by pain.

She closes the book and slips into sleep.

Greg and Al are mostly silent on the way back to the American sector. The day has been long and emotional. Both men are weary. But Greg cannot resist asking, "What do you think? Will we ever figure it out? Will there be time enough in this life to make sense of it all?

"I don't know." Al sighs. "Until then, I guess we will just have to learn to love life more than the meaning of it."

He looks off into the shadowy horizon and mutters: "I'm not a religious man, but I seem to remember a line from the Old Testament. Something about 'in the fullness of time'."

"In the fullness of time, man will receive his just reward," Greg fills in.

"Amen!"

"Yeah …Amen!"

*****

The winds of summer 1945 brought home from the war the early waves of American GIs. In all, over eight million men and women from 55 theaters of war and four continents eventually returned.

Al Jergowsky and the other men aboard a converted Liberty Ship will get their glimpse of the Statue of Liberty today. Most were up early that morning to see, not only Bartholdi's sculpture, but the great land mass they have been dreaming about since they left. As the ship steams, slowly past the grand matriarch there are a few cheers – but mostly silence. Tears of joy flow unashamedly from thousands of eyes. Every combat veteran experiencing the same feelings and weeping collectively.

The first time Abram Dzierzgowsky sailed under the figure of Libertas, he was a toddler held in his parents' arms. The future was unsettled then. They were strangers in an alien land. There was only hope and no guarantee that dreams were real and not mad delusions. "We will live and we will see." That was the only promise that these newcomers could hang their lives and their futures upon.

This time, Al is coming home! And the optimism is unbound.

19. "The Destroyer of Worlds"

The same month Al's ship brought home its cargo of troops, the United States dropped the atomic bombs on Japan. Mercifully, the Japanese surrendered a week later. The War Department estimated an invasion of Japan would have cost over a million US casualties. Purple Hearts cast for the impending attack went into stockpile. They were minted in such numbers that they were available for issue for the next seventy years.

An open letter to *The New York Times*, read: "The first atomic bomb destroyed more than the city of Hiroshima. It also exploded our inherited, outdated political ideas." The co-signers were US Senator J. W. Fulbright, Owen J. Roberts of the Supreme Court, and Albert Einstein. In his memoirs, J. Robert Oppenheimer who headed the Manhattan Project quoted words from Hindu scripture:

> If the radiance of a thousand suns
>
> Were to burst at once into the sky
>
> That would be like the splendor of the Mighty One.
>
> Now, I am become death, the destroyer of worlds.

Well before the end of 1945, the high-minded idealism that appeared in editorials, academe, and speeches before parliaments and congresses was yielding to real-world politics. Richard Barker-Jones' fears for the future were taking form. The casualties to truth were mounting. Although the conclusion of the Second World War officially ended hostilities, it set in motion new conflicts with old and new casts of combatants and hatreds. The questions that haunted Barker-Jones foreshadowed the future, and loomed above a war-ravaged world that had not yet picked its head up from the misery.

Jews returning home found no home to return to. In Poland, despite the efforts of heroic Polish Gentiles who risked their lives to save Jewish ones, the scale of plunder of Jewish assets gave rise to an entire economic class. An unfamiliar bourgeoisie took the place of murdered Jews. In the countryside, Jews were taken off trains, stripped of their possessions, and murdered forthwith. Communists would later exploit deep-seeded antisemitism via its ranks of government apparatchiks and the police.

In other parts of eastern Europe, survivors fared no better. The Czechs created the Revolutionary Guard. The RG was nothing more than a herd of thugs with authorization to brutalize at random. With the support of officials in government and the army, they led mobs into the street stoning Germans and arbitrary "suspects" they believed to be collaborators. An entire family of innocent Swedes fell victim to the madness.

The British government had blood on its hands as well. Churchill's government pacified detained Cossacks who had fought against Stalin with promises of being folded into the British Army and reassigned to Africa to defend the empire. In June of 1945, however, Royal troops handed them over to the Soviets to face their fate as traitors. They resisted by forming massive human mounds of men, women, children, and priests praying, singing psalms, holding crosses and icons. At a roundup along the Drava river in Austria, some drowned themselves in the river. Others hanged themselves from trees. The remainder ended up in cattle cars headed east.

The British also delivered to Tito the Croatians who had opposed him. They, too, were regarded as traitors rather than POWs. Forced on a death march with their hands tied behind their backs bounded with wire, they starved, when not bayonetted, shot, or beaten to death. Their bodies lay on the roadside or cast into ditches. A witness to the mass graves recorded: "Because the blood started to soak through the ground, and because the ground started to rise due to the swelling of dead bodies, the partisans covered the soil with an alkaline solution, more soil, and then leveled the ground with tanks."

While the vanquished suffered under the oppression of defeat, the victors struggled with inconvenient and unsheathed truths about their victory. Gentiles in German-held territories drew false equivalents between their anguish under occupation and the victimization of Jews. The claim, "We suffered, too," was a common assertion. In a former Dutch resistance paper, a letter to the editor included these lines: "They [Jews] should be constantly mindful of their duty to be grateful. They are not the only ones who suffered." Duly, in 1950 the first memorial to the Holocaust appeared in Amsterdam. It is called: "The Monument of Jewish Gratitude."

In London, Poles who fought valiantly at Monte Casino, the Falaise Pocket, Market Garden, and in the air for the Battle of Britain were banned from marching in the victory parade. Churchill did not want to offend Stalin. They were betrayed again at the San Francisco Conference by being excluded. Poland found its place on the outside looking in beside Germany and Japan, as delegates from 50 Allied nations crafted the United Nations Charter. At the same time events in San Francisco unfolded, 16 leaders of the Polish resistance were being tortured in Moscow.

While Germans averted their gazes and covered their noses at the sight and smell of black and bloated human remains at Bergen-Belsen, movie-goers in Allied cities also repulsed at the images. Films revealing the atrocities in the camps were distributed to the Allied home front. Often, audience members attempted to sneak out only to be forced to return to the theater. An account from the *Daily Mirror* read: "People walked out of cinemas all over the country and in many places there were soldiers telling them to go back and face it." An English soldier reaffirmed Barker-Jones' burden of history: "It is everybody's duty to know."

In the US, representatives met to sign agreements to establish a global system for international commercial and financial relations. The Breton Woods Conference drew delegates from 44 nations. Their meetings created a blueprint for a new post war order to foster growth, cooperation, and a mechanism to help constrain the scourge of war. The establishment of the International Monetary Fund and the International Bank for Reconstruction and Development occurred in the conference rooms of the Mount Washington Hotel. Bretton Woods became the site because Democrats in the US Senate needed to appease a Republican senator from the state of New Hampshire. The Mount Washington Hotel was chosen because it was one of the rare hotels in rural America that accepted Jews. Since Henry Morgenthau was the United States Secretary of the Treasury, the limited options for him and other participants made the decision convenient, obvious, and necessary.

Klaus Haas returned to a nation in ruins, destitute, and looking for scapegoats. Former soldiers were viewed with suspicion and tainted by the tint of shame and defeat. The same citizens that cheered their real and imaginary military victories now leveled contempt at the establishments responsible for the final humiliating downfall and unutterable crimes. The Nazis were to blame for everything in a country where now there were no Nazis to be found. Germans stepped forward offering to conduct the execution of war criminals. Some volunteered, others wanted compensation (based on an amount per each head). The cost of racist nationalism to Germany was 5 million lives, universal opprobrium, partition, and Soviet oppression. By the time of its re-unification, generations of Germans had paid their tribute in shame, anguish, and tears. And still, the cancer that lead to their catastrophe percolated along the fringes of German society stoked by militant neo-political social groups.

For the United States, there was no scent of defeat. The country bathed in the glow of its victories on the European and Pacific fronts. The veil of invincibility blinded the country to its limitations, drove defense policy, and helped pull the US into engagements around the world. Korea, Cuba, Vietnam, Cambodia, Dominican Republic, Lebanon, Grenada, Kuwait, Panama, Somalia, Bosnia, Iraq, Afghanistan, Libya, Syria represent a litany of wars and adventures across the hemispheres – some just, some ill-advised and ill-fated.

America's national security policies more than suggest a muffled echo of John Adams' dark allusion: "Power always thinks it has a great soul." Waves of descendants of what was referred to as "the greatest generation" would bear the onus of US hegemony. And, by their sacrifice, fill veteran hospitals with their broken bodies and cemeteries and urns with their remains.

20. The Jersey Shore

The ocean breeze plays with the flags and banners at the 1958 Annual Memorial Day Jamboree. Legions of kids in Cub Scout uniforms, Pop Warner equipment, Little League uniforms, and cheerleaders' outfits swarm the grandstand of the old racetrack. Pip Feeney wipes the crust from his eyes while he tries to get a fix on where he is. "Why am I looking at an army of kids?" Pip had spent the evening with some horse trainer pals swilling at their favorite trough, Manny's Hawaiian Palms Cafe. The last thing he remembers is breaking into Dorothy Johnson's house and washing the old dowager's dishes. That must have been sometime this side of midnight. Instead of going home to the Jergen's farm, where he boards his horses, he came back to the track. Now, the mission is to find his car and escape unnoticed. Who knows what other crimes he may have committed last night? Dusting the furniture? Polishing the silver?

Meanwhile, the racetrack hums with frenzy. Scoutmasters and coaches are eager to show off the skills the children have learned after a year of practices, meetings, drills, and field trips. All this work is meant to give the parents some hope that their sons and daughters are trainable. For most, the attempt fails every year, but anticipation and promise are always high. The day never disappoints. In fact, it is glorious.

"Well, if it isn't the Jergowskys, Or, I should say…Jergens."

"Hey Rip. How's it going?"

"Well. Al…Helen."

"I heard from Judge Morton there was a SNAFU at court when you were there to change the name."

"Right. After the legal items were done, Bill had to formally ask the boys if they agreed to the new surname."

"And the little one refused!" grumbles Helen.

"What! Why?"

"Davey thinks Jergowsky is a better name for a football player. He thinks it will help him in his career!"

"All the boy talks about is playing for the Baltimore Horses."

"It's the Baltimore Colts, Honey.   The Baltimore Colts."

"Whatever. With all the team logos he has in his room – the place looks like a tack room."

Rip Wagner cannot control his big smile. "Well, like my father would tell people. 'It's hard to beat a boy that makes you laugh.'"

"I couldn't believe how stubborn he got. Thankfully, he gave in – after a half hour. Speaking of boys that make you laugh, where is everybody?"

Rip points to a section of the grandstand a few yards away. "The poker club? Just over there."

"Why so far away from the action?"

"Doc Demarest's little girl is with the Mighty Mite cheerleaders. It seems that the voice and pitch of 45 seven-year-old girls is lethal. Doc wants to stay out of the kill zone. Is David with his Pop Warner crew?"

"No. He got recruited by his Cub Scout den. I think they are putting on a boxing demonstration."

"Interesting. What weight class is he?"

"Actually, he's a turnbuckle this year."

"Ah. It's hard to find a good one these days."

"Oh, and he is one of the best!" Al says with a chuckle. "We'll see you back at the seats."

The proud parents and friends take their places as the opening ceremony commences. Mayor George Woolley welcomes them and begins his annual address. Being Mayor of Oceanport, New Jersey, is mostly ceremonial. George is almost eighty. No one has much motivation to vote against him, or run against him, despite his struggle with premature senility. Mayor Woolley governs with benign neglect. It is an effective approach to managing the town's expectations.

"Before I turn the festivities over to the children and their wonderful…err…ah wardens, let's all rise and sing one of my favorite songs: You're a Grand Old Fag!"

"What did he say?"

"He must have meant: 'You're a Grand Old Flag'."

"Are you sure?"

The high school band churns out George M. Cohan's gaudy march. The crowd responds with raucous voices and applause. "Let the games begin!" shouts Mayor Woolley.

Immediately, the track infield explodes into a virtual free-for-all. The Pop Warner Mighty Mites run plays against an imaginary team, as the replacement players wrestle each other on the ground. Some use tackling dummies as opponents. Sammy Magno and Bennie Klein smash their helmets together to see if they can get their face-guards to interlock. After fifteen minutes of relentless head-butting – success!

The little leaguers show off their baseball skills. Teddy Maley is covering centerfield. He pulled his team t-shirt over his head and re-set his cap on top. Balls whiz by him while he stands motionless and oblivious to the projectiles. His teammate in leftfield, Jimmy Kerney, has a different technique. When balls are hit anywhere in his direction, he instinctively runs in circles screaming. Chubby Schley roams right, until a stray mutt looking for a kid to play with seduces him.

At David Jergen's (Jergowsky's) boxing exhibit, a turnbuckle has gone missing. Mrs. Garippo, the saintly den mother, is in a panic. She scans the infield for her missing cub. Tommy Korhonen has found an open patch of turf where he stands and periodically leaps up in the air. He seems to be imagining an Olympic unsynchronized jumping competition.

"Tommy dear, we need you at the boxing matches."

"I can't stop now. I'm ahead 6 to 4!"

Louise breathes in and smiles fondly. "I understand. Good luck, Dear." She immediately marches off in the direction of the Pop Warner and Little League teams. There is almost a one hundred per-cent chance she will find a coach happy to donate a small warm body – as long as Louise returns him to his owners.

In the stands, parents, aunts, and uncles laugh and cheer with abandon. Doc Frisch turns to Mario Foggia and says, "I guess what they say is true. 'Behind every successful person stands an aston-ished parent'."

Above them flies an enormous American flag. When the wind lifts it just right, it folds into an exaggerated red, white, and blue smile. Like a proud parent, it seems to say: "Aren't they beautiful!"

Helen Jergen is laughing, and wiping the tears from her cheeks. "Where is Al?" she asks herself. "He never misses a game, a school open house, or a father and son event. He practically lives for them. I don't want him to miss this. It's not like him to not be here."

Helen leaves her friends to find her husband. She passes the concession stands and goes to the parterre area. Maybe he went back to the car for something. She might be able to see him crossing the lot. When she turns a bend – there he is. Al has found a secluded corner and is leaning against the railing. His body is bent over the top rail and his head is in his hands. She can see by his trembling shoulders he is sobbing.

"Al!"

"I'm fine…I'm fine."

Helen rubs the back of his neck. She does not know what to say. She has always seen the stable, durable side of him. Now is his time. She allows him space, and has her own memories of war and tragedy. Helen's brother was with a bomber crew. Like many others, he did not return.

Since he came home, Al never discussed the war. Helen does not know the names of a single man Al served with, or the names of the towns in France, Belgium, and Germany where he fought. He never told her about the carnage, or about the friends he had and lost.

She does not know that the sight of starving and dead children comes back to haunt him sometimes when he is at a little league game or chaperoning a field trip. During his time with the occupation army, he had to live with scenes of children's bodies riddled with bullets and blown apart. He cannot forget the children in the camps and on the streets living in filth reduced to skeletons. The little frightened and dead eyes peering everywhere searching for their parents or just asking, "Why?"

For both, it was always about looking and moving forward. This was their America now. America did not want to look back. There was too much ahead for her. The future held so much hope – it seemed so big. A British Labour Party leader complained: "The US was simply too rich, too unscathed, too powerful."

"Would you rather be alone?" she asks.

He pauses before responding. The weight of conflicting emotions mix with the flashbacks. The sight of these kids is moving, inspirational. They are the embodiment of freedom and innocence. "But can we ever protect them enough?" Al worries.

He also wonders, "When is it a time to move on?   When is it a time to remember?"

"No …No, I'm fine." He assures her. "Let's go back."

As they rejoin their friends, the brutal memories begin to fade. Life is normal, happy. Al can hear his son's excited voice above the crowd. David sees his father through the mass of kids and adults. He comes running towards him overflowing with energy and proudly yelling, "Dad! …Dad!   Did you see me? …Did you see me?"

*****

The years pass, and the dream continues. From an immigrant's small son to the typical American success story. Al has had his hard work rewarded. He has watched his sons grow and believes nothing is beyond the reach of their grasp. Not because of their extraordinary skills or talents, but because anything is possible.

David listened when his father said to him, "If people who come to this country and think things will be automatically easier, they will be disappointed. The US was founded for those who can build something, create, and who are not afraid to fail. If you are willing to imagine and take your chance, this country will support you with all its might. I didn't say that. Hamilton did. Don't trust me. Read him."

Al never wore a flag pin on his lapel. There was no red, white, and blue bunting draped under the house windows on the Fourth of July. When it came to patriotic displays, his manner was non-decorative. He held it inside. It was in the form of a parapraxis, or Freudian slip. Often times when he waxed philosophically and spoke of life, he was actually referring to America. To him, the two words could be interchangeable. America and life, both express for him a vast range of possibilities.

By most standards, he has succeeded in life.

It is a bleak January night now, and Al is looking out the window of his hospital room.   From his warm bed, he can sense the intense cold just on the other side of the window. He never liked the winter. His tolerance melted away after the Ardennes. That was 34 years ago but he still remembers the time outside Schmidt trying to fight off the punishing cold by hugging the make-shift furnace inside his tent. There were the frozen bodies, the knee-deep snow, and the unrelenting wind that could break your heart.

Al was never the type of man to relive the past. But now, lying in recovery from his third heart attack, it is a good time to reflect. As he thinks back, the radio softly plays songs from the Big Band era. In the background of his thoughts is Tennyson whispering, "I am all that I have met."

It would be easy to indulge in self-pity. He is also recovering from pneumonia. He has felt weaker and drained in the last few years. But tomorrow he is going home. He can continue, again, with whatever God or life intends for him.

Despite the early struggles, he survived. There were losses, but the returns eclipse the costs. Coming to America as a small child, growing up in anti-Semitic neighborhoods, surviving the Great Depression, only to be sent back to Europe, into the greatest conflict in history. After the horrors, the perils, and the lost friends, he faced the tasks of rebuilding his life and various businesses. Not only did he attain the American Dream, he was able to pass it on to his sons. The oldest, Robert, is on staff at the hospital where Al is recovering. The youngest is working for a doctorate. David keeps his head above water by working at the family business. Al chuckles as he thinks, "I wonder if Dave realizes he's the lowest paid employee on the payroll? Maybe when I get back, I'll consider giving him a raise."

Al smiles to himself. "I am more than content. I am grateful." Before he drops off to sleep, he thinks back on his father. It was he who brought him to American. He is the reason his boys are Americans. "This country is the only reason I survived and thrived. It owes me nothing." Al closes his eyes and slips into a deep restful sleep. He has earned it.

At 6:45 A.M., 40 miles south of Al's hospital bed, Robert awakes. A crushing pain is strangling his chest. He struggles to get a breath but cannot. He is unable cry out. The intense pain makes him helpless and hopeless. Even though he has no medical conditions, he is sure he going to die – now!

At that same time, 30 miles north of where Al lay, David awakes with the same symptoms. The torment is unbearable. "Oh God! Let me die. I will if this pain doesn't go away!" David has enough self-possession to think, "I've been worried about Dad, and now I'm the one dying of a heart attack. Maybe, that's for the better. What would the world be like without him in it?"

David's prayers for the pain to stop are finally answered. Immediately he falls into a solemn, bottomless sleep. There is nothing but the dark and a welcoming feeling of freedom. Fifteen minutes later he awakes. He lies silent and still. "What just happened?" he asks. Something inside him lets him know the world has changed – but how?

The phone in the kitchen rings. One of his roommates answers. Dave knows whom it is for.

David pushes himself off the bed and moves to the outer room to take the receiver. It is Dr. Frisch: "Dave…He's gone." There is only the silence. "I'll stay here with your mother until you get home."

David hangs up the phone. It is over. "I shared his pain and the last moments of his life. At least…I was there with him. A closing farewell. My last connection with my father…"

21. A Chance Encounter

Back at the old barracks in Carlisle, David Jergen has fought off the pull keeping him drawn to the picture in the adjacent room. He completed his notes and delivered his conference presentation. It is breakout time and a chance to meet with colleagues and audience members. This is time to address follow-up questions, exchange cards, and maybe learn something.

Academe is not the exclusive realm it once was. The unbridled growth that began in the 1960s made it a haven for specialists who feel the need to shield themselves from the real world. The standard of scholarship suffered. Tenure only degraded the field further. Ivory towers became networking institutions, hives for armies of administrators, and reposes for politicians and misfits. In 2010, apresident of a major US university remarked, "The worst thing to happen to a school is to win a national football or basketball championship."

The United States created the greatest research infrastructure in history after the war. A new class of business managers and owners, scientists, policymakers, and researchers propelled the country to its finest era. It still attracts first-rate scholars, but they labor beside bilious social re-toolers, bureaucrats, and hacks. The lowering of academic standards from kindergarten through high school has not done much to prepare students to think critically either. Grade inflation at elite universities has made employers require college entrance aptitude scores rather than transcripts from their applicants. There is not the same quality of true experts as there once was. Most academics are random points of light. Many are dim, shining on preconceived conclusions, untruths and then devote their research to working backwards. The private sector grant system is often as interested in corrupting and exploiting research as it is in commercializing it. The exorbitant costs of education and the "corporatization" of higher education has left the best intentions compromised.

Arthur Edward Todd is an outlier. He is well-known as an author and as a devoted teacher. He has held posts at several US and European universities. His fluency in German and his dual doctorates in political science and psychology have made him a dean in his field. Now a Professor Emeritus at Purdue, he travels, attends conferences, and accepts invitations to speak. Tonight, he is at a series of lectures at the Army War College in Carlisle, Pennsylvania. The main speaker is Dr. David Jergen. The topic is, "US Post-Cold War Defense Strategy: A Country at War with Itself."

Over a buffet, Professor Todd and David Jergen meet and have a moment to exchange stories and compare notes. An automatic friendship strikes up despite the age difference. They discuss the conference, but once the shop talk winds down the discussion becomes chummier.

"I always enjoy reading you, Dr. Todd. You have a way of throwing facts at us with an additional wider lens. And the cryptic humor doesn't hurt. I gotta ask, though – does your American perspective play as well in Germany?"

Todd allows himself a slight chuckle. "Well, let me put it this way. Bismarck was quoted as saying: "God has a special providence for fools, drunkards, and the United States of America." If he is right, I would guess that would buy me some license."

"And the Germans do like beer. So, what led you to become an expert on Germany? Was there a personal connection, or did you simply fall into it like many of us do in our fields?" asks David.

"I was there during the war. It was my first time away from home, and the experience turned me into a different person. It made me rebelliously curious." Todd smiles. "Dorothy Parker once said: 'The only cure for boredom is curiosity.' And there is no cure for curiosity.' There was the GI Bill, and as long as the country was willing to invest in me…" Professor Todd shrugs. "Why not?"

David smiles back. He now unleashes a soft laugh. "Dorothy Parker. So that's where my father got that quote."

David goes back to the conversation. "My dad was there during that time, too. Funny, since I was only nine years old he told me to 'Join the Navy'."

"Your father was in the Navy?"

"No, actually. I remember asking him one day, 'Why do you want me to join the Navy? You were Army.' He said because in the Navy, 'Before you get killed, at least, you can get a shower'."

By that day in David Jergen's childhood, the Second World War had been over for more than a decade. He knew his father's caustic humor. Yet, he remembers how, at the time, there was no suggestion of comedy or lightheartedness in his father's voice.

He goes on. "I was too young to understand what he meant.   I just took everything my father told me as gospel – whether it made sense or not."

Dr. Todd chuckles sadly. Unceasing dreams of hot showers, flush toilets, soft beds became obsessive at the front. These creature comforts would never be taken for granted again swore the Dogface. As such, the old soldier shares a common fatalism with a young stranger.

"So, you were Navy, eh?"

"Just Officer Candidate School, in 1972. No combat experience." Dave admits. "Unless you consider the U.S. Government the enemy."

"Well, at least you didn't run up to Canada or go to Sweden."

"No. My plan to dodge the draft was to enlist."

"That was shrewd. Did that ploy work out?"

"By the time I reported to Newport, Vietnam was over and so was the draft. After several months of screaming and yelling, the Navy put us on inactive reserve."

"Your father must have been proud." Dr. Todd grins.

"Oh yeah. At least I delivered on that dream he had for me."

"So where did your father serve during the war?"

"France, Belgium, Germany…He was at Hürtgen."

Professor Todd's eyes become cheerless. He falls silent for a moment and looks down. Todd shakes his head and whispers something that only he can hear…something suffused with almost inexpressible grief.

"Hürtgen," he repeats. "Where is your father now?"

"Dad passed away years ago. He and my mother are both at Arlington."

David keeps talking, not recognizing Ed Todd's change of mood. "Like I say, he never talked much, but he kept his regimental journal in the library. I remember reading his unit was the first Allied unit to cross the Rhine."

Ed Todd arouses from his melancholy. His voice becomes accusatory for the first time. "My unit was the first unit to cross the Rhine! What unit was your father in?"

David is taken back. "Not sure. They were re-attached several times, but I think his division was the 78th. His regiment might have been the 311th.

Dr. Edward Todd's eyes begin to well up. "What was your fathers first name?"

"Al."

"Al. Al Jergen," Todd echoes quietly. "There were so many, so many whose faces are still clear as day, but their names long forgotten. And others whose names I remember, but can't see their faces."

"Dad was in the Medical Corps."

"The Medical Corps." Repeats Dr. Todd. He shakes his head. "Those guys were our guardian saints. You know the Army tried to cut their pay, because the medics were not considered combat troops? They would have, too, if the rest of us didn't protest. They had the highest mortality rate at the front. They even went with the wounded into the POW camps to make sure they got proper treatment."

His mind goes back to the concerned officer at the aid station who listened when he opened up about his fear of never getting back to normal life again. He recalls asking: "Am I going to remember this day for the rest of my life?" He cannot remember if they exchanged names, but the memory of the officer and their conversation remains. Their meeting seemed a conclusion to a story of an unforgiving and wretched place and time. He never knew what happened to that lieutenant. That question lingered throughout the years as the continuity of the war years became inseparable from the arc of his life.

The other flashbacks return: the grotesque sight of a pair of arms rising from the earth clutching a tin pot full of urine. The day at Schmidt when he caringly handed off a wounded German to death. The dead trooper waving goodbye as his corpse is carted off the battlefield. The time he sat with the mutilated girl on her way to the aid station. He never learned her name, or her story. But her blood soaked through to his skin and he cannot forget the smell when it dried.

"I wish I could tell you more about my Dad's army experience. I wish I knew more." David humbly admits. "In fact, I wish I knew half as much about him as he did about me." David tries to pass off the comment as a flippant remark, but it is the truth, and it stings.

"That's alright, David. I know enough. I wish I'd met your father, but he sounds a lot like a good man I did know."

Ed Todd looks on at David Jergen. He can see the sadness in David's eyes as he remembers his father.

"David, I was in the 78th. And my regiment was the 311th. I didn't know your dad, but I can tell you this – your father was a hero."

David is silent. All he can do is nod. A sense of loneliness engulfs him. He does all he can to hold back tears.

Later that night, back alone in the guest room, David Jergen sits in a chair rubbing his neck. As he massages his stiffening muscles, it reminds him of his father's habit. Whenever he was frustrated with a problem or irritated by someone's endless prattle, David's dad would reach behind and knead the area above his upper back. The memory almost lightens his mood. But the melancholy refuses to release him.

At that moment, David's gloom is disrupted by a knock at the door. He sees his brother standing in the doorway. David has not seen his brother in over a year. David is happy to see Robert despite the ageless, and sometimes snarky, sibling rivalry. Their differences are as stark as their likeness.

"Good lecture. I'm glad I came out. I really enjoyed it," Robert commends his brother.

"Good. I'm glad you made it. And it's good to see you." David nods back.His big brother's energy level has always been higher and his confidence more unbendable. As the less assertive brother, David was drawn into a career of academic research. Rummaging through data and arriving at conclusions that always left the door open for alternative positions and provided an anodyne existence compared to the world outside. Academia is a world awash with alternative solutions and opinions. This was a welcome release from his childhood. Growing up, not just any answer was acceptable.

It was particularly true when something went wrong or expectations fell short. His Dad's favorite phrase and overhanging warning, C'est plus qu'un crime, c'est une faute ("worse than a crime, is a mistake"), were words of pure dread to David's ears. To his father's further agitation, his youngest son's response was always, "Huh?"

and, eventually, "...Uh, what does that mean, again?" Another learning moment wasted.

Robert, on the other hand (and to David's frustration), claimed he was not familiar with the phrase. He recalls falling down and always being told by his father to "Get up!" If he groaned over a tummy ache, his Dad was there to tell him: "You're not sick." He also remembers that he was right. And in the times when Robert really was hurt or sick, his father knew and never left his side. Neither of the boys ever rebelled. Why would you, against the person who loved you more than anything else?

"Here's the picture I wanted you to see." David walks his brother into the anteroom.

"All last night I thought about that German medical kit we had in the house. I didn't really notice it when we were growing up, until you told me what it was. Dad never talked about it with me. I never thought to ask how he came by it. I only remember his saying you never took souvenirs from a battlefield. It was bad luck. Plus, souvenirs off dead Germans were not something you wanted to be found with if you got captured. What do you know about it?"

"He told me this story about a truce during a battle near the German border when he gave it to me. That was just before I left for med school. He was a triage officer. When the American and German medical teams separated, a German doctor offered it to Dad as memento. Other than that, I remember he mentioned an army photographer was there taking pictures, making notes, and even drawing sketches. I don't know much more. It must have been a mad scene. Trying to save the GIs and then turning around and saving lives of the same people who a day earlier were trying to kill you."

David nods and adds, "I looked up Dad's service record in the archives yesterday. Do you know he was awarded the Bronze Star and the Purple Heart? The archivist told me his service uniform would have included at least ten battle and campaign ribbons. He just left them behind. The guy in the archives said a lot of combat veterans never collected their medals. They didn't want them."

David and Robert exchange glances, but not a word. Their silence says everything. Robert breaks the hush. "That triage officer could have been him – focused, commanding, purposeful."

"Don't forget exacting," says David. "Remember when he helped us with our homework? I was glad to go back to school and face the teachers. The classroom was a lot less stressful than being tutored by Dad."

"But, you have to admit, it paid off," Bob reminds Dave.

After another round of chit-chat, both brothers know it is time to move on. Dave walks Bob to the doorway. As they approach the door, Robert notices the rosary piled on David's desk. He stops and looks back at his brother. "You keep his rosary with you all the time?"

"Always," responds David.

They shake hands and give each other soft embrace.

"Will we see you around the holidays?"

"I'll be there."

Hours after Robert leaves, his father's story continues to plague David. At the same time, he senses something new growing up inside him. He has learned a lot the past two days. But still, there are so many gaps. If only he knew more. It might allow him to know the man his father was, and also allow him to learn something about himself.

David rises from the chair and walks to his work desk. He opens the window and lets the fresh air circulate inside the room. Outside, a lithe autumn rain is sweeping over the trees and pavement. From his window, he can make out the rooves of the officers' quarters. He can see the distant flickering of villages nestled in the Cumberland Valley. He smells the aroma of the nightshade as he looks out on a narrow sliver of his vast country. No words come to mind, only a remote feeling of hope, guilt, and an odd malaise over his lingering innocence and over the innocence he lost.

22. Bless me Father, for I Have Sinned

A December snowfall is settling over a small town on the New Jersey shore. The rooves of houses, tops of cars, and the heads of villagers take on a downy coating. A sense of peacefulness drifts over the amiable park and the half-frozen lake. The white adorns the shops and hides the grime, muffles the sounds of traffic. Children make snow angels while mothers keep handy their thermoses of hot chocolate. One little boy is off on his own. He marvels at the way the freezing air turns his breath into puffs of light vapor.

The hamlet is becoming whiter, quieter...softer. In the background, the bells of the church overlooking the lake toll 3 o'clock. The gentle storm offers a momentary pause for lives accustomed to whirling traffic, the pressures of work, and garish light. The snow is turning Winter Lake, New Jersey, into a Currier & Ives holiday tableau. But the skies are becoming darker, suggesting that an angrier storm might be approaching.

David Jergen takes in the scene and dreams about his own spent childhood: going to ballgames with his father, the summer cookouts on his family farm, the simple pleasure of sitting on the floor around the fireplace with the family dog – always having a safe place to return when tired, sick, or just lonely. He takes a deep breath, looks up at the massive iron church doors, and ascends the stairs.

Inside, the pews are sparsely dotted with worshipers. The line for confessions is abandoned, except for a lone older woman and her walker. Upon his turn, David steps inside the "dark box." He kneels.

"Bless me Father for I have sinned. It has been thirty years since my last confession."

There is nothing but silence from the other side of the screen.

"I confess bearing hatred in my heart for the ones responsible for my son's death and for the authorities who refused to prosecute the case. There was pressure on them from the press. But politics kept them from doing their job. Not only can I not rid myself of this hatred, I have even come to welcome it. At best, I might forgive others for myself. If so, I forgive them for the infinite suffering in my heart. But the sufferings of my child, I have no right to forgive."

David takes a moment to calm himself, then continues. "In addition to these mortal sins, I confess doubting my faith and wanting revenge. I demand justice now, Father, not in some infinite time and remote space."

There is an audible moan and then a command. "Tell me something about your son."

Dave cannot help letting out a low groan. With his anger momentarily staunched, he goes on. "Clay was the toughest, sweetest kid there's ever been. In most ways, he was more like my father than me. His mother abandoned him when he was a child. Still he spent his life trying to please people, making them smile. He was bright, successful. He was working on Wall Street when it happened. His boss flew in from London to be with him the night of his funeral. His teammates from Fordham, high school, Pop Warner flew in from everywhere. I had seen people from my own life I had not seen in decades. I was known as Clay's father sometimes more than by my own name."

David realizes he is letting go of the things he has been wanting to say out loud. He seldom admitted his pride in Clay. He let others boast. Now, the chance to speak adoringly about his son feels like a fitting confession, not a sort of self-praise.

"Among his things, we found his rosary. It was a gift from my mother. Just before he died, I think he was looking for answers. He left us before his life was about to take off and before he was about to find peace in the world. I carry his rosary with me wherever I go. It's always with me and I can't part with it."

David stops to regain his strength. He struggles to keep from stuttering. "Six...six months after Clay died I...I over-dosed on my medication. I was rushed to the emergency room...the same hour one of the boys responsible for his death was being released from prison. He was going to a welcome home party."

David takes another deep breath. "The medication I took, I have been taking for over twenty years. I have to wonder: Was I truly unconscious of the mistake I was making? As the police once told me, 'There are no such things as coincidences'."

"Go on, please."

David slumps. With his hand he rubs the back of his neck before continuing. "I don't believe I am suicidal, but I am not afraid of death either. Life frightens me more. The best moments of my life were the time spent as Clay's father. I just should have had more time."

David closes his eyes and rubs his forehead. "I want to be absolved in the event of another future… 'mistake' committed unconsciously or…." He stops. After a long pause he mutters, "For these and other sins, I confess my guilt."

A short silence, and then the priest assigns David his penance. "For your penance say one Gloria Patri. And know you and Clay are in my prayers."

With his confession complete, David speaks more freely. "Father, I cling to this anger and my distrust of authority, willfully. Will there be a day when I am more forgiving, less flawed, and granted the grace and strength I should pray for?"

"Yes, my son."

"But when?"

"In the fullness of time, we all will find peace."

David Jergen recites the Act of Contrition and leaves the confessional. He stands by a font, and looks up at the suffering image hanging from the cross above the tabernacle. He turns his back and walks through the somber metal doors into the world.

The park is quiet. The children have disappeared. The evening is growing colder, and the night is getting deeper. David walks home, alone.

When he arrives, the house is still. He turns on the light, throws down his coat, and plunges onto a leather couch. David rests quietly, pondering the future. For several minutes, he thinks and feels nothing. Trapped between a distain for life and his damned base instincts, he feels a numbness overtaking him. With Clay gone, he has lost everything. At least nothing can ever happen to him now. But that sense of freedom is pitiful compensation for the loss. His soul is still filled with gloom. No release could ease the anguish in his heart.

Through the gloom and doubt, David notices a large box in the next room seemingly waiting for him.

He pushes himself off the sofa and enters his small study room. Carefully, he separates the packaging. It is from his brother, Bob. He unwraps the package. Before him is the same print that held him captive in the guest room at the barracks at Carlisle.

The picture, "A Time For Healing," faces across from him, again. Suddenly, the memory of his father reminds him of the value of loving, and of being loved. "Love is such a power. You never fully appreciate its strength. I draw from it every day," Hedzia told Richard Barker-Jones at Belsen.

The thought of his father trying to save the lives of men who had tried to kill him, the love David holds on to for both Al and Clay – Will he learn to draw on it? Can a life actually be enriched by pain? As someone once wrote, he asks himself.

David Jergen walks over to the computer sitting on the desk. Before he begins to type, he takes Clay's rosary from his pocket and places it next to him. David is determined to research his father's war. He would look into that haunting picture many times, and he will learn who that lieutenant really was. Maybe he will find that "thing to live for," and, perhaps, in the fullness of time, find the peace he achingly seeks.